SAWYER

Susan Fisher-Davis

Men of Clifton, Montana

Book 18

Erotic Romance

Sawyer Men of Clifton, Montana Book 19
Copyright © 2021 Susan Fisher-Davis
First Print Publication: October 2021
ISBN: 9798752133404
Cover Artist: Untold Designs Romance and Fantasy Covers
Cover Model: Daniel Kennedy
All cover art copyright © 2021 by Susan Davis

PUBLISHER: Blue Whiskey Publishing
Webpage: https://www.susanfisherdavisauthor.weebly.com

Acknowledgments

To my betas, Renee, Alison, and Holly—you ladies are the
best, and I love all of you.

To my husband, Rob—you are the best.

To Daniel Kennedy for being Sawyer.

You can find Daniel on Instagram at:

@strong.f.kennedy_

To the ladies in my Facebook group: Susan's Hot
Cowboys—you make it fun.

As always to you, my readers.
I wouldn't be able to do this without you. I love
each and every one of you
and I appreciate your support.
From the bottom of my heart, thank you.

If you, or someone you know, suffers from domestic
violence and would like help, please contact The
National Domestic Violence Hotline at 1-800-799-
7233 or visit,
https://www.thehotline.org

Dedication

To my friend, Sandra Swann Rathwell, who passed away October 2021.

I will miss her every day.

Rest in peace, Sandy. I hope to see you again one day.

Prologue

Piper Howard glanced over her shoulder to see Cory running behind her as she ran down the hallway. She let out a scream when he grabbed her hair, stopping her. He spun her around and slammed her against the wall.

"Pip, when are you going to listen to me?" he asked as he put his face close to hers.

"Cory, please," she whispered and hated begging him for anything.

"Please, what? You know you deserve it, Pip."

Just as he moved back from her and raised his hand, she kicked him in the groin, making him fall to the floor. She ran to the bedroom, slammed the door, locked it, and backed into the corner. She was petrified, and her entire body shook as she waited. She screamed and jerked as he kicked at the door.

"I am going to kill you this time, you fucking bitch," he yelled through the door as he kicked it.

Looking around for something to protect herself with, she saw her cellphone on the nightstand, but just as she picked it up, the door flew open, and Cory ran at her. He knocked the phone from her hand and backhanded her. When she fell to the floor, he straddled her, wrapped his hands around her throat, and started choking her.

Piper clawed at his arms as panic set in. He squeezed until she was sure she was going to die. She looked up into his face to see a menacing grin, then her world faded to black as she passed out.

She jerked awake to see nothing but darkness.

Had she died? Turning her head, she saw her alarm clock and let out a relieved breath. The clock showed it was two in the morning.

When Cory snored beside her, she stilled for fear of waking him. God, she hated him so much, but she was so scared to leave him. He would kill her for sure.

As she lay there, tears rolled down her temples and into her hair, and she placed her hand over her mouth so he wouldn't hear her. She had to do something. She couldn't live like this. She had to take that chance.

She glanced over at him to see him with his back to her, so she slowly lifted the cover, slid from the bed, and stood. She stared down at him and wished she could kill him.

She took a deep breath and got on her knees to look for her cellphone. She moved her hands along the floor because there was no way she would turn on the light. Her hand ran across her sneakers, and she picked them up. When she found her cellphone, she got up and slowly headed for the door.

When he rolled over, she slipped to the floor, set her cellphone down, put her hand over her mouth, and held her breath until she heard him snore again.

She didn't want to waste time trying to take any of her things. Not that she had much. He never let her buy anything, and he sure as shit never bought her things. The only thing he gave her was misery and pain. She was done. If he woke up and saw her trying to leave, he would go into a rage, and he was such a violent man, but she had to try. *She had to.* The closer she got to the door, the more terrified she became.

Dear God, please let me get away from this horrible man.

Making it to the door, she was thankful it wasn't closed, but she quietly pulled it shut behind her and dashed down the hallway to the front door. She quietly picked up her keys and purse and opened the door. She looked back to the closed bedroom door, stepped out, closed the door, and ran to her car in her bare feet.

She was shaking so much that she had trouble putting her key into the lock. There was no way she would use the fob because she was so scared that he'd hear it. She took a deep breath and inserted the key, opened the door, got in, closed the door, and hit the locks. If he came out, there was no way he was getting in this car. She pulled her shoes on, tied them, started the vehicle, put it in gear, and drove out of the driveway with just the clothes on her back.

She headed for her Aunt Evie's place. Piper knew Cory would know that's where she'd go, but she would be gone before he even got there. She had a head start on him. Hopefully, he'd sleep until his alarm went off. He had a job to get to, so she hoped that would give her time.

Piper knew what she had to do, and luckily, she'd been offered a job in Clifton, Montana, which Cory knew nothing about. The letter was with her aunt. Piper had given it to her since it arrived. Cory didn't know she had a post office box, and it was a good thing because he would have beat her for sending out resumes and getting mail about job offers.

Once she arrived at her aunt and uncle's place, she'd let them know where she was going, and she knew they would never tell Cory. They knew she lived in fear but not the extent of it. They had begged her to leave him, but she'd always been too scared.

"Not anymore. I'm leaving you, you gutless pig, and I pray to God that I never see you again."

Chapter One

The day started early on a ranch. Any ranch, but it seemed to Sawyer Griffin, he'd just gone to bed when the alarm buzzed from the nightstand. Reaching over, he slapped the top of the clock radio to turn off the irritating sound. Tossing the sheet off, he swung his legs over the side of the bed, rubbed his eyes, and pushed to his feet. When he stretched, he winced when he heard his bones crack. He was getting too old for this shit.

He picked up his boxer briefs, jeans, and T-shirt from the chair beside the bed, then headed to the bathroom to shower. Flipping on the light switch, he blinked against the brightness and made his way to the shower. Reaching inside the stall, he turned the water on, then stepped in when it was warm enough. Damn. *Was* he getting too old for this? God knows he loved what he did, but there were days he'd be happy to stay in bed.

"You're only forty-three, Griffin. Still considered a young man," he said and snorted. "Yeah, to who? Someone in their seventies?"

He reached for the shampoo, squirted some in his hand, rubbed it on his head, scrubbed his hair, rinsed it out, and then cleaned his body. After shutting the water off, he opened the shower curtain, grabbed a fluffy blue towel, rubbed it over his head, dried off, wrapped it around his waist, and stepped from the shower. He walked to the sink and swiped his hand across the steamed-up mirror so he could see to shave.

After applying the shaving cream to his lower

face, jaw, and neck, leaving his mustache alone, he put his razor under the water and started shaving. He stopped and leaned close to the mirror.

"Son of a bitch. Another gray hair," he muttered as he put the razor down and moved his hand through his hair as if it would make the gray disappear. The hair at his temples was gray, and he'd learn to live with it. But, now in the front? Grinning, he thought about his father always saying it was white paint in his hair.

The smile left his face when he realized he hadn't seen him in over a month. That was just wrong. They were close. They always had been. Not that he didn't have time to see him; his father lived in Arizona. He needed to send him a quick text and tell him he'd call him later.

Frowning, Sawyer knew he needed to get in touch with him to give himself peace of mind that he was all right. Blair Griffin was in his late sixties and in good health, but you never know. His father had also been a vet, and his sons followed in his footsteps. Sawyer built the hydrotherapy rehabilitation on the ranch, but his father was the sole owner of it.

Once he finished shaving, Sawyer wiped the excess cream off his face, splashed on aftershave, dressed, and made his way to the kitchen. He flipped the light on, sauntered to the K-cup machine, inserted a cup, pressed brew, and waited.

The pet door flap opened, and his German shepherd/Husky mix dog Rio stepped inside and ran across the kitchen to sit in front of his master. Sawyer stared down at the dog and grinned.

"Where have you been?" He reached down and rubbed the big dog's head. He chuckled when Rio tried to get closer.

Sawyer turned to get his coffee when he heard it sputter to a finish. Taking the cup from under the spout, he picked it up, blew on it, took a sip, and walked to the door to peer out. It was going to be another hot day if going by the haze, but he'd be too busy to notice.

There were five horses he needed to get into the pools. Four had muscle strains, and one had arthritis. He hoped he didn't have trouble with any of them, but sometimes a horse freaked a little when first led into a pool. Though most horses loved the water and knew how to swim, two handlers would hold the leads as the horse made its way through the water. Swimming helped their muscles. Just as it helped people. Though water therapy was used on many animals nowadays, he only worked with equines.

There were six pools to use and three water treadmills. Both were very effective in helping with sprains, arthritis, sore muscles, or lameness. Sawyer had been doing it for years, but it took a while to catch on in the area. Once the local veterinarian, Dr. Tessa Garrett, started sending patients to him, he was so busy he barely had time to think.

Some were skeptical at first, but they soon realized hydrotherapy was very beneficial to their animal. It brought horses that competed in many events to his ranch, from reining competitions, barrel races, rodeo events, polo, and vaulting. Most horses in the area ended up coming to his ranch if they had problems.

It was something he loved doing. He had read about it in college and decided that was what he

13

wanted to do once he received his DVM degree. After he opened his practice in Bozeman, he got his certificate in equine rehabilitation. With that certificate, he could work with trainers, farriers, and owners to reach a common goal of healing the horse from illness or physical distress with no surgical intervention. After evaluating the animal, rehabilitation therapists used various healing modalities to help the horse fully recover from musculature, nervous system, and joint ailments.

Sawyer also owned an equine hospital in Bozeman that specialized in rehabilitation. When his father told him he wanted to move to a warmer climate, Sawyer decided it was time to come home to Clifton, Montana. It took him two years to get the place ready for clients. Once he did, he began working towards the goal of having his ranch be the place people could bring their equine, and he'd do what he could to help them before resorting to surgery. It was an excellent plan, and it took off like wildfire. At first, he only had two pools until veterinarians from connecting states sent patients to his ranch. He had to hire people to help him and had four more pools installed. His ranch had an excellent reputation.

Each pool had a large commercial filtering system that kept the water clean. The chlorination and PH systems kept the water free of bacteria. The water was tested daily to ensure its quality and safety. One of the pools was a straight-line design where the horse swims against resistance. The other four were circular. The pools were the safest method for swimming equine patients since they are only a few strides from safety should they become distressed or unable to swim. Two straight-line pools were in-ground, and decks surrounded the circular ones. The largest pool was both straight-line and circular. It was only used when a horse was doing well enough to swim on its own.

Once he finished his coffee, Sawyer rinsed the cup, placed it in the sink, and headed for the door. He took his hat off the peg, slapped it on his head, opened the door, strode to his truck, climbed in, and headed for his office in the barn.

****

"What is wrong with you, Frick?" Piper stopped the horse and rubbed her hand down the front shoulder to his knee, making the horse step back from her.

She sighed and left the stall to look for Bonner. She boarded her two horses on his ranch because she couldn't spend a lot on a home, and finding a place with a barn was out of her price range. She had been lucky enough to find a house to rent where she could also board her horses.

Making her way down the barn's aisle to Bonner's office, she knocked on the door. It opened, and Bonner Gentry smiled when he saw her. He was a very handsome man with dark hair and light green eyes. Standing at six five, he was much taller than her, even though she was a tall woman at five nine.

"Hey, Piper. What can I do for you?"

"I think Frick is in pain," she said.

A frown marred his brow. "He was fine yesterday. Let's go take a look."

He stepped out of the doorway and followed her to Frick's stall. Bonner entered and walked around the horse, looking at him.

"Where?"

15

"I think it's his right shoulder. He won't put any weight on that leg and pulled away from me when I ran my hand down over it."

Bonner nodded and ran his hand down the horse's shoulder and his leg, and Frick snapped at him, making Bonner jump back. He grinned at Piper.

"I believe you're right."

She laughed. "Good thing you're fast on your feet."

"I'm glad I am too. It could be arthritis. Frick's almost twenty-three years old. Horses get arthritis, as we all do. Let me call Tess and have her come out. She might give him a steroid shot or recommend hydrotherapy."

"Hydrotherapy? I've heard of it but is there a place close by that does that?"

"Yeah, Dr. Sawyer Griffin has a ranch just for that purpose. You can't find a better equine rehabilitation therapist."

"Okay, let's call Tess first and see what she says."

Bonner nodded, walked from the stall, and motioned Piper to follow him back to his office. He called Tess then told Piper she'd be here within fifteen minutes.

"Stephanie is out, but you're more than welcome to wait in the house or in here. Since Tess will be here soon, I don't see any reason for you to go home and come back. I have some things I need to take care of, then I have to leave to get some grain cut."

"If it's all right with you, I'll just hang out in the barn."

"Yes, ma'am. That's fine." He gave her a nod then strolled out of the office.

16

Piper watched him leave, then took a seat on the sofa to wait for Tess. Piper had met Bonner's wife, Stephanie, at the Clifton Diner when she first moved here from Wyoming. She had been in Clifton for two months and was looking for a place to stay before bringing her horses here. Luckily, her aunt and uncle kept them for her until she got settled. She had told Connie, the diner's owner, she hadn't found a place yet, since the apartment complex had no vacancies, and though the Dalton Motel was nice, the stay was getting old. Connie offered the apartment above the diner, but Piper was hoping to find a place close to where she could board her horses. Stephanie overheard them and offered her a home to stay in on her ranch, and she could also board her horses there. Piper had cried and pulled Stephanie into a big hug.

She just hoped she didn't have to run again. Cory would be looking for her, of that she had no doubt. She pulled her cellphone from her pocket and did a little reading while she waited for Tess.

"Hi, Piper. Bonner said there was something wrong with Frick."

Piper looked to the doorway to see Tess standing there. Getting to her feet, Piper put her phone back into her pocket and smiled.

"Yes, he won't put weight on his right front leg. I'm not sure if it's his shoulder or his leg."

"Well, let's take a look." Tess moved out of the doorway, and Piper led her to the stall.

"Be careful. Frick snapped at Bonner," Piper said.

"Oh, I will. I know how these big boys can be." Tess moved into the stall and placed one hand on the horse's face and the other on his shoulder.

"I don't feel any swelling in his shoulder, but that doesn't mean anything." She ran her hand down his leg, and he stepped back from her. "I think it could be his knee more than anything."

"Bonner said he was fine yesterday."

"He probably sprained it when he was running or something. I'd recommend taking him to Dr. Griffin's ranch. He's good."

"Bonner mentioned him. No shots?"

"I'd rather try the hydrotherapy first. We'll try a steroid shot if Frick doesn't respond to the therapy, but I think the water will help him. It's amazing what that water can do. You know it helps us humans, and the horses love it. Sawyer has pools and treadmills for them. He'll know what to do. He's a wonderful therapist." Tess reached into her medical bag, pulled a card out, and handed it to her. "Here is his address and phone number. He's close to here. Maybe you'd like to go there to see it first. If it's not something you want to try, get back with me, and we'll go from there."

Piper took the card, looked at Tess, and nodded. "I'll just ride out there. I'd love to see it."

Tess grinned at her. "It's an amazing setup. Let me know what you want to do. Unless you have any more questions, I'll get going. I'm meeting Sam for lunch."

"No, no questions. Have a great day, and thanks so much, Tess." She added the address to her cellphone.

"No problem. It's my job. See ya," Tess said, waved, and left the barn.

Piper strolled out of the barn and into a blast furnace. The sun was high and beating down. Dust wafted up from her boots as she made her way to her truck. Opening the door, she climbed in, started the vehicle, then drove out of the driveway. She reached over to turn the a/c on, but it didn't help. Hell must feel like this. The GPS told her to turn left and travel for ten miles. The two-lane blacktop was empty as she drove to the ranch. Heatwaves rose in the distance like invisible flames.

After driving the distance, the GPS told her she had reached her destination, and she pulled into a driveway. A closed gate sat in front of her with a *No Trespassing* sign on it. She noticed arrows pointing to the right of the gate, so she followed them and pulled up to a small cabin that had *Office* written on it above the door and a neon *Open* light in the window. After pulling into a parking spot, she opened the door and stepped out. She put her hand above her eyes and glanced around but didn't see anyone. She saw five barns in the near distance.

She took a deep breath and pushed the door closed on her truck, walked up the steps, and entered the cabin. A pretty brunette sat behind a counter and smiled up at her when she walked inside.

"It feels so good in here," Piper said with a smile.

"It's horrible today. I'm Peta. What can I help you with?"

"I'm Piper Howard. Dr. Garrett suggested I come by and check out the facility. She thinks my horse has a sprained knee, and hydrotherapy would help. I'd love to see how it works."

Peta smiled. "Of course. Let me call someone to come and get you. They'll take you to the barn."

Piper nodded as Peta picked up the phone and made a call. When she hung up, she smiled at her.

"Trevor will be here in a minute."

Piper frowned. "Trevor? I thought his name was Sawyer."

"Trevor is one of the workers. Sawyer is the vet."

"That's fine. I don't care who shows me around." She laughed.

A big grin lit up Peta's face. "Trust me, you won't mind which one of those two show you around."

Laughing, Piper took a seat on the bench to wait. It wasn't long before the door opened, and a very handsome cowboy entered. He glanced around and smiled when he saw her. Damn. He was gorgeous but probably in his mid-twenties. He put his fingers to the brim of his hat.

"Trevor, this is Piper Howard. Ms. Howard, this is Trevor Ward."

"Ma'am. I understand you want to see how this place works?" Trevor smiled at her.

Piper got to her feet. "I do if you have time."

"We always have time for potential clients. Come with me." He looked at Peta, and Piper saw him wink at her and watched as the young woman's cheeks turned pink.

He held the door for Piper, and they walked out into the heat. He led her to a UTV then opened the passenger door for her. She climbed in and sighed as the air conditioning hit her skin. The driver's door opened, and Trevor got in.

"I didn't know ultra-terrain vehicles had air conditioning."

"Few do, but the doc thought this would be the best type to have since clients like to see all the facilities. Not just the hydrotherapy pools but the pastures and such."

She nodded. "Makes sense."

"This thing probably cost more than my truck,"

20

he said with a chuckle.

Piper laughed. "Mine too." She glanced behind her. "And it seats four."

"Yes, ma'am."

He pulled up to a barn and came to a stop, making Piper sit up and glance around. Looking over at her, he nodded for her to get out, then met her at the front of the vehicle.

"We'll go in this one first. I think the doc is in here."

"All right."

Trevor opened the door to the barn and held it while she entered. She came to a stop and looked at everything in front of her. Two large circular pools with decks around them sat beside each other but a reasonable distance apart. Each had two workers holding lead ropes while walking around the deck, leading a horse around making it swim against a light current. She looked at Trevor.

"How many pools?"

"Six pools and three treadmills. Two barns have two round pools each, and one has a very large straight-line/circular pool, and the other has a straight-line pool along with three water treadmills."

"I thought I saw five barns."

"Yes, ma'am. The fifth barn is where the clients' horses are kept until they're brought over here and put into stalls to wait for treatment."

"Makes sense. This is an amazing place," she murmured.

Trevor jerked his chin for her to follow him. She glanced around with a smile on her face. This might help her horse.

When she spotted the man, she came to a

complete stop. She stared at the good-looking cowboy leaning against a set of metal steps used for the workers to get to the walk, which surrounded the top of the pool. He stood with one hip cocked, and his arms were folded across a very impressive chest. A white straw cowboy hat sat low on his forehead, and dark hair peeked out at the back. His T-shirt was blue, and the sleeves wrapped around impressive biceps and dark hair covered his muscular-looking forearms. Her eyes traveled down his chest to his waist, then down to his jeans. She bit her lip to hold back a groan. Those jeans hugged him like a second skin and left little to the imagination. On his feet were well-worn, distressed cowboy boots. Pulling out the collar of her T-shirt, she blew a cool breath down toward her breasts. She hadn't been this affected by a man in...well, ever, and it surprised her she could even think that way, considering what she'd left behind in Wyoming.

"Ma'am?"

Mentally shaking her head, she tore her eyes from the sexy cowboy and looked at Trevor.

"Sorry. I was just watching the men lead the horse around." She knew damn well her cheeks were flaming.

Trevor nodded and continued. She did her best to keep up with him, but she couldn't stop herself from looking at that cowboy again. When she ran into the back of Trevor, she knew her cheeks were on fire when he spun around to look at her.

"Are you all right?" he asked her.

"Uh, yes. I'm sorry. I wasn't paying attention."

"It's all right. Let me introduce you to the doc, and he can answer any questions you have about how it works."

"Can't you?"

"Some of it, but Dr. Griffin has a degree in equine science, and he knows more about a horse's health than any man I know. Come with me."

She followed him and inwardly smiled when she saw he was heading back for the sexy cowboy. *Oh, yeah. If this was the vet, she'd talk to him about anything.* She kept her eyes on him as they approached and watched as he glanced their way and straightened up. He didn't take his eyes off her as she strolled to him, and she watched his eyes roam over her from head to toe. She had never had a man look at her the way this one did, and she was on fire.

"Hey, boss. This is Piper Howard. Ms. Howard, this is Dr. Sawyer Griffin."

"Ms. Howard, it's nice to meet you," he said, sticking his hand out, and his deep voice sent shivers down her spine.

"Nice to meet you, Dr. Griffin." *Was that her voice all breathless?* She put her hand in his and felt a shot of lightning.

"Please, call me Sawyer."

"Piper."

"I appreciate you helping Ms. Howard, Trevor. Take your lunch. I know it's time for Peta to take hers."

Piper looked at Trevor to see his cheeks turn red.

"Yes, sir," he muttered, turned on his heel, and quickly made his way to the door.

Piper looked back to Sawyer Griffin and thought she'd never seen a more handsome man. He was very tall, and she figured he had to be close to Bonner's height. His dark hair looked so soft that she had to curl her fingers into fists to keep from reaching out to touch it. She could see gray in the hair on his temple, and there were crow's feet at the corners of his eyes, and those eyes were gorgeous. They were grayish-blue. She had never been a mustache fan, but his was great. Not too bushy. She'd put him in his early forties. *Just right.*

"Those two think I don't know about them. I know *everything* that goes on around here," Sawyer said, chuckling.

"I noticed he winked at her when he came to get me at the office."

"Yeah, he hightailed it out of here when we told him someone was at the office who wanted a tour."

Piper laughed. "Young love."

Sawyer nodded. "So, what can I do for you?"

Anything you want. Damn, a man was the last thing she needed right now...or ever.

"Dr. Garrett thinks my horse, Frick, could benefit from hydrotherapy. She thinks he sprained his knee. He's not young, so I'm sure he has some arthritis too. He's almost twenty-three. I have his brother, Frack too, but he seems fine even though he's nineteen."

"Frick and Frack?" Sawyer asked with a chuckle.

"I didn't name them, but I didn't want to change their names."

"I can understand that. I'm sure Frick could benefit here too. Tess wouldn't suggest it if she didn't believe in it. Come on, I'll show you around." He looked up at the two men on the walk. "He's done for the day. Get him some extra oats and put him in a stall. I'll be around here somewhere."

The two workers nodded, and Piper watched as they moved the horse over toward a ramp that had a rail across it. Another man removed the gate, and they led the horse up the slope. When he shook his body, water flew off and landed on the men. Piper laughed as the men tried to cover up. Sawyer chuckled.

"Happens every time."

"Do you ever get horses that won't go in?"

"All the time. I have a horse of my own that won't even walk through a puddle. He'll jump it every time."

"What do you do with those, then?"

"We use the treadmills for those stubborn ones."

She could not keep her eyes off his ass in those jeans as she followed him. He could be an advertisement for the brand because he filled them out better than any man she'd ever seen. *Damn, the heat in the barn was stifling.*

They made their way through the barns, and she asked a million questions because she loved the sound of his voice, and when he spoke, a dimple peeked in his right cheek. God! She loved a five o'clock shadow. Sideburns met the stubble at the lobes of his ears, and she noticed quite a few strands of gray in those sideburns. His lips were perfect, with a bowed upper lip and full bottom lip. What would he think if she just wrapped her arms around him and nibbled on that lip? She snorted, and he turned to look at her with a raised eyebrow. Clearing her throat, she shook her head.

"Are you married?" he asked her.

"No."

"Engaged? Involved with anyone?"

"None of the above. What about you?"

"No, ma'am, I'm divorced. I asked because I wanted to see if you'd like to meet for lunch but didn't want to piss off anyone you could be involved with. We can talk about getting your horse here if you're interested." His eyebrow rose.

"Oh, I'm interested," she said. *Oh my God! She'd never been so brazen in her life.*

When he grinned, showing perfect white teeth under that mustache, she was sure she burst into flames.

"I'm happy to hear that. Let's get some food. Have you been to the Clifton Diner?"

"Yes. I love their burgers."

"Then let's head there. I'll have one of the guys take you back to your vehicle. I have a few things to do first and let everyone know I'm heading for lunch. I can meet you at the diner in about twenty minutes. Will that work for you?"

Nodding, she turned away and strode to the door. She was sure he was watching, and when she glanced over her shoulder to look, his lips rose in a slow, sexy grin. *Oh, my.*

****

Sawyer watched her leave and took a deep breath. *Holy hell. What a woman.* He couldn't take his eyes off her sexy ass as she walked away. Piper Howard was one beautiful woman, and he wanted to know her better. He'd held his breath when he asked if she was married or involved because he was hoping she wasn't. Her wheat-colored hair was up in a ponytail, but it was short, so her hair probably just touched her shoulders. He'd still love to take it down and wrap his hands in it to pull her close. Her blue eyes sparkled with mischief. And when she said she was interested, he wanted to take her to his office and talk her into having sex on his desk. He frowned as he thought she looked

26

familiar, but he knew he'd never met her before. He wouldn't forget meeting her, that was for sure.

Turning, he headed for his office while pulling his cellphone from his pocket. He called Peta to let her know he'd be gone for a while after he finished some paperwork. He grinned when she sounded out of breath. No doubt she and Trevor were somewhere together.

A little while later, he pulled into the parking lot at the diner and found a place to park. Shutting the truck off, he headed for the front of the diner. He reached for the handle just as it opened, and his good friend, Jake Stone, walked out. He held the door for Sawyer.

"Hey, Sawyer. How are you?" Jake asked as he put his hand out to him.

"I'm good, Jake. You?" Sawyer shook his hand.

"Too full to move right now." Jake chuckled as he rubbed his stomach.

"Those burgers smell fantastic," he said.

"You know they are."

"I didn't realize I was so hungry until now. I'm meeting someone here about getting her horse to the ranch. Tell Becca I said hello."

"Will do. Enjoy your lunch." Jake strode off.

Sawyer entered the diner, and everyone waved or called out to him. He gave them a nod, glanced around, found Piper seated at the counter, and made his way to her.

"How about we grab a booth?"

"Sure," she said as she hopped down from the stool.

Sawyer stared at her and dropped his gaze to her lips. When she took her bottom lip between her teeth, he almost groaned. He wanted to nibble on it. It surprised him he was interested in this woman. Sure, he had seen women for sex since his divorce. Hell, he was a man, but Piper had him thinking more along the lines of seeing her for more than that.

They weaved their way through the tables to a booth in the back. He waited for her to slide in before he did the same across from her.

"Hey, Piper. Sawyer."

He looked up to see Lanie Donovan.

"Hey, Lanie. How are you?"

"Wonderful. Do you two need menus?"

"I don't. Just tell Owen I'll have my usual, please. Water is fine."

"I think I'll have a burger with lettuce, onion, mustard, and tomato. Onion rings and water, please, Lanie," Piper said.

"Separate checks?"

"Yes, please." Piper nodded.

"You got it. I'll be back with your drinks." Lanie turned and moved away.

"Lanie is so nice." Piper smiled.

"All of them are. Have you met her sisters and cousin?"

"Yes. Deidra, Rissa, and Sloane. I also met Stephanie Gentry here, and she offered me a place to stay on her and Bonner's ranch."

"Do you board your horses there too?"

"Yes. I couldn't afford a big place, but I wanted to move here. I stayed at the Bur Oak guest ranch a year ago and fell in love with the area. Have you lived here all your life?"

"No, I lived in Bozeman until a few years ago, but I was born and raised in Clifton."

"Any children?"

"I have a daughter. You?"

"No. I was in a relationship for two years. The worst time of my life." She blew out a breath. "It's a long story."

"I understand."

"How long have you been a vet?"

"About seventeen years now. I attended Oregon State University, and after getting my degree, I bought a small hospital in Bozeman. After getting the hospital up and running, I took courses to work in equine rehabilitation. When Dad wanted to move from the ranch, I knew I wanted to come back home and get the practice up and running here. I knew there wasn't one close to Clifton."

"So, that makes you what? In your early forties?"

"Forty-three."

"I'm thirty-five."

"I figured you were in your late twenties."

"Well, thank you. How old is your daughter?"

"Brooke just turned twenty-two. She's attending the same college I did. Following in her old man's footsteps to become a vet, just like I did."

"Wow, you're not proud at all." She laughed. "How long were you married?"

"Twenty years. We were both twenty when we got married."

"That's a long time."

"Yeah, maybe I'll tell you about it one day, over dinner." He grinned when he saw a blush move across her cheeks.

A few minutes later, Lanie set their dinners in front of them, smiled, and walked to another table. They picked up their burgers and took a bite. When Piper moaned, Sawyer almost choked on his.

"Good?" he asked.

"Better than sex," she said, smiling.

"Want to bet?" He watched as heat poured into her cheeks.

"A little cocky, aren't you?"

"Nope. Just confident. You let me know when you want to take that bet, Piper. Anytime."

Her head tilted, and she stared at him.

"I'll do that." A slow smile lifted her sexy lips, and he wanted to reach across the table, grab her hand, and drag her out of the diner. He really wanted to get to know her.

"So, no men in your life now?" he asked.

"Nope, and I'm really not sure I want one." She shrugged.

"Your relationship was that bad?"

"Yes. Like I said, it's a long story."

"Mine too, but I'm glad it's over."

"I'm sorry. I see so many who are happily married. Especially around here."

"I'll give you that one."

"Typical man."

"Piper, I am anything but typical."

She cupped her chin in her hand. "You know, I believe you."

"I was in, what I thought, was a good marriage until three years ago. Like I said, it's a long story."

"Maybe we can share those long stories sometime."

"I'd like that. I just realized now why I thought you looked familiar. Anyone ever tell you, you look a little like Faith Hill?"

"Yes. I don't see it, but I've heard that."

"Well, you do. Your features resemble her." He didn't take his eyes off her.

"So, tell me how you think the hydrotherapy will

help Frick."

"We'll either get him in one of the pools or the water treadmill. The water gives them a slight resistance to move against. It won't hurt them or give them more pain. Just like with people, it helps with arthritis. Some horses love the pools, while others will only go into the treadmill booth."

"How does that work, exactly?"

"Most horses are used to going into closed spaces, like trailers, so leading them into the booth is no problem. Once they're in it and start walking, we fill it with water up to their knees. Then we add more water. Up to the tops of their legs and raise the speed a little. After a few minutes, they seem to love it." He grinned.

"It makes sense that it would work. When my aunt broke her hip years ago, her doctor suggested swimming to help her, and it did. I suppose we don't realize how much resistance that water makes." Piper smiled at him, and he had an absurd desire to kiss her senseless.

After eating, Lanie appeared with the checks, and Sawyer took them both.

"I can pay for my meal."

"Not saying you can't, but I invited you to lunch, so I'm paying." He leaned back in the booth, folded his arms, and grinned. "You could invite me to dinner."

Piper copied his pose. "I could, could I?"

He shrugged. "Don't see why not." He leaned forward and placed his arms on the table. "I'd like to see you again."

"You will when I bring my horse to you." She grinned.

"Wow. Shot down." He shook his head.

"I'll fix you dinner one night. How's that?"

"Tonight?"

"No," she said, laughing. "But I do want to get to know you."

"Well, I'm all for that." He gave a brief nod. "I can wait."

"Good."

"I need to get going and get my ass back to work. Do you want me to pick your horse up at Bonner's?"

"You'd do that?"

"Sure. I've done it before for patients. It's no big deal."

"I'd appreciate that."

"Consider it done. Any day you want to visit the ranch, feel free."

"I'll do that."

He slid out of the booth. "Can I get your number?"

As she slid out, she gave it to him.

"Thank you for lunch." She spun around, walked to the door, and out of the diner.

After placing a tip on the table, he walked to the counter to pay for their lunch, and Connie stood there at the register. He reached into his back pocket for his wallet and handed her cash to pay for the two meals.

"Did you have a good lunch, Sawyer?"

"Yes, ma'am, as usual. Thank you."

"I'm glad you enjoyed it. Piper is such a sweet person."

Sawyer narrowed his eyes as he looked at her. But she wouldn't meet his gaze.

"Are you matchmaking?"

"Me? Would I do that?"

"In a damn heartbeat."

Connie burst out laughing. "You know me too well. But she is lovely, don't you think?"

"I do, and that's all I'm saying. Keep the change, and have a good day." He touched the brim of his hat and walked out the door. He smiled as he heard Connie laugh behind him.

She was right, though. Piper was a sweet person, but she was hot as hell, too. He liked her, and he had just met her. She was tall, and he'd always had a weakness for that since he was so tall at six foot five. He was looking forward to seeing her again and getting to know her, but something seemed to be holding her back. Maybe it was because of her failed relationship. He wasn't sure, but he hoped to find out. It surprised him he was interested at all, especially after the fiasco with Marcia. Shaking his head, he made his way to his truck and drove back to the ranch.

****

Piper drove home with a smile on her face. Sawyer Griffin was a hell of a man. She'd thought so when she first saw him, and now, since spending some time with him, she liked him. He was not only very handsome, but he had a great sense of humor. She loved a man who could make her laugh.

"What ended a twenty-year marriage? I'd love to know about the relationship he'd been in," she muttered.

She laughed when she thought about him telling her to let him know when she wanted to take that bet. Wouldn't she love to do that? It had been a while since she had sex; she wasn't sure she remembered how to do it. She bet Sawyer could certainly remind her. His body looked to be in great shape. She pulled the collar of her T-shirt out and flapped it to try to cool herself down. That man had her burning up. Cory had never pleased her. *In. Any. Way. Ever.* All Cory ever did was use his fists. She knew not all men were that way, but she was so scared to try again. Cory never hit her before they moved in together, although there had been signs. His temper always scared her, but it wasn't until they moved in together that she found out just how bad his temper was. She just hoped he didn't find her because she knew he was looking for her. He'd never give up on finding her, and it scared the bejesus out of her.

Did she even want to take a chance getting to know Sawyer? Sure, he seemed like a nice guy, but so did Cory at first.

She shook her head. She just didn't know. The thought of getting involved with a man, *any* man, was so terrifying to her. What if Sawyer *was* like Cory? She gasped. Was that what happened to his marriage?

Shaking her head, she didn't think so because he said he'd tell her about it, and she was sure he wouldn't say he hit his wife.

"Could lie about it, though," she muttered as she drove home.

Chapter Two

The next morning, Sawyer drove his truck, pulling the horse trailer behind it, onto Bonner's ranch. He stopped by the barn and stepped out. The sun beat down hot on his shoulders even though it was early morning. Shoving the door closed, he headed for the barn and entered it. After letting his eyes adjust, he made his way down the barn aisle to look for Bonner.

Horses stuck their heads over the stalls to see who the new visitor was. Sawyer stopped at several of the gates to rub their soft noses. As he turned to head further into the barn, he saw Bonner and Stephanie in a steamy embrace, kissing. Sawyer grinned when he saw Bonner's hands slide down over her backside and tug her closer. Sawyer cleared his throat and chuckled when they sprang apart.

"Hey, Sawyer," Bonner said with a sheepish grin.

"Bonner. Stephanie. I didn't mean to interrupt, but I'm here to pick up Frick and take him for some therapy."

Bonner grinned, kissed Stephanie again, then she walked past Sawyer with a smile on her beautiful face. It was good to see her happy.

"Nice to see you again, Sawyer," she said as a blush moved across her cheeks.

"You too, Stephanie." He touched the brim of his hat.

Bonner put his hands on his hips as he watched Stephanie walk out of the barn. Then he looked at Sawyer and jerked his head for Sawyer to follow him.

"Come with me. He's back here. I'm hoping the therapy helps him. Piper told you he was twenty-two, right?" Bonner asked him.

"She told me he was almost twenty-three, so I'm sure he can benefit from it," Sawyer said as he glanced around. "She told me that Frack didn't seem to have any problems getting around."

"No, he seems fine. I laughed when Piper told me their names, but she said she didn't name them."

Sawyer chuckled. "I hear some weird names."

"I bet you do." Bonner led him to a stall, stopped in front of it, and nodded toward the horse standing there.

"Here he is," he said as he rubbed the horse's neck.

"Hey, big boy. How are you feeling today?" Sawyer murmured to the big roan quarter horse as he touched his velvety nose. The horse blew in his hand.

"He's a good horse. Very gentle, but Piper said he's slowing down lately. I'm hoping the therapy will help him." Bonner patted the horse's neck.

"Me too. I'll do what I can." Sawyer took the lead rope down from beside the stall, opened the gate, hooked it to the halter, led Frick out, down the aisle, and loaded him into the trailer with Bonner following him.

"How's it going at the ranch, Sawyer?" Bonner asked him.

Sawyer closed the door on the trailer, leaned against the side of it, and folded his arms.

"I'm busy as hell. I love it, though. I enjoy seeing the animals benefit from the water. Brayden brought a horse over last week. Poor thing is in

36

terrible shape. Someone mistreated him, and he's real skittish, but I'm going to work on him a little at a time. His knees are in awful shape. I might adopt him myself," he said with a grin.

Bonner chuckled. "Why am I not surprised to hear that?"

Sawyer pushed off the trailer. "I have no idea."

"Yeah, sure you don't." Bonner grinned, making Sawyer laugh.

"I'll get this big boy to the ranch and see if I can help him. See you later, Bonner."

Bonner gave him a salute, then reentered the barn. Sawyer climbed into his truck, fired it up, and drove home.

He stopped at the office to see if Peta had any messages for him. Pulling the truck to a stop at the gate, he left it running to keep it cool. He strode across the gravel, climbed the steps, and entered the office. He sighed as the air conditioning hit his hot skin.

"Peta?" he called out.

She came from the backroom and smiled up at him.

"What's up, boss?"

"Just wondering if I have any messages?"

"Oh, yeah. A few." She walked to a corkboard, took his messages down, and handed them to him.

Scanning through them, he frowned when he saw one from Marcia. *Damn.* He would not call her. Looking through the rest, he saw she had called two more times. Flattening his lips, he scowled as he stared at her number.

"She called quite a few times. I quit writing the messages down," Peta told him with a shrug.

"I sure as hell won't call her." He blew out a

frustrated breath, crumpled the papers, tossed them into the trash, and turned to leave. When he reached the door, he looked back to Peta. "Any new patients?"

"Of course. I don't know how you even stand some days. You have to be exhausted."

Sawyer grinned. "I have great help."

He winked when she gave him a big grin, then he walked out the door, closing it behind him. He climbed back into his truck and drove to the barn where he kept the animals before working with them.

He backed the truck into the barn, and after shutting it off, he walked to the back of the trailer.

"Hey, Doc."

Sawyer turned to see Trevor heading toward him.

"Trev, open stall twelve, please, and I'll get this big guy in there."

"Sure," Trevor said as he turned, jogged down the aisle of the barn, and opened a gate.

Opening the trailer's door, Sawyer stepped in, rubbing his hand along the horse's back as he did.

"You're going to love it here, Frick. I promise I'll do all I can to make you feel better," he murmured to the horse.

Frick turned to look at him, and Sawyer stopped moving then laughed when the horse took his hat off his head and swung it around.

"Give me my hat or no water for you," he said as he reached for his hat, but Frick was having none of it and kept it out of his reach. Sawyer huffed, shook his head, and after untying the lead rope, he had the horse walk backward out of the trailer with his hat between his teeth.

"So he's a hat thief," Trevor said with a laugh.

"Looks like it. I'll get it once we get him in the stall. I hope so, anyway."

"Remember that horse that took your hat, threw it down, and stepped on it?"

"Shhh, don't give this guy any ideas. Although, a lot of horses like to take your hat."

"Probably just because they can. He's a gorgeous horse, though."

Sawyer agreed. The big roan had a red coat with fine white hair, but his legs, mane, and tail were black.

"He is, but I have a feeling he's going to be mischievous."

He heard Trevor laugh as they made their way down the aisle, with Sawyer leading Frick and wondering how his hat would look once he got it back.

****

Saturday evening, Piper sat in the recliner, aiming the remote at the TV and flipping through the channels. Blowing out a big sigh, she placed it on the arm of the chair, leaned her head back, and closed her eyes. Sawyer Griffin's face appeared behind her eyelids. Damn, that man was fine. She wondered if he picked up Frick yet, and if he did, she hoped he could help the horse. Horses could live up to thirty years old, but if Frick had arthritis, he'd need help to control it. Sawyer seemed to love horses. Why else would he have a place to help them as much as he could? Any man who helped animals was a good man.

Cory was not a good man. He hated animals, but he loved to belittle her regularly, and when he wasn't doing that, he was hitting her. The first time he hit her, she'd been so shocked that she ran to their bedroom and started packing to leave, but he beat her so badly that she couldn't open her eyes. He swore he'd never let her leave him. The only way would be in a pine box.

One night, when he was out of town, she went out with the girls. When she got home, it had surprised her to see that he had returned early. He sat in the living room, in the dark, waiting for her. When he turned the light on, the blood drained from her face as she watched him get to his feet and fist his hands. He called her horrible names and told her she was never allowed out without him again. She'd been a little tipsy and laughed. That had been a big mistake. He beat her so severely that she thought he had broken her jaw. She was terrified of him. The thought of even trying to leave him made her sick to her stomach because she knew he'd never let her go, and she was too afraid to tell anyone. She had lost her job at the hospital because she missed too much work, but there was no way she could go in to work with her face all puffy and bruised. For two years, she lived with a man who scared her more than anything else in the world. She'd rather stare down a rattlesnake.

The last time had been the last straw. He'd gotten angry over *her* letting him run out of beer. Anything would set him off, but after trying to strangle her to death, she knew she had to go. She was lucky that he had stopped once she passed out.

She traveled to her aunt and uncle's place to let them know where she was going and borrowed money since she didn't have any. She left that night and drove until she reached Clifton. She hoped he'd never find her, but Piper knew he would never stop

looking. Her aunt and uncle would never tell Cor
where she was, and neither would her parents
They had never liked him, and she should hav
listened when her mother told her she didn't hav
a good feeling about him. Her father would hav
killed him if he'd known how Cory beat her. Sh
had been too embarrassed to tell them. Even he
Aunt Evie didn't know all of it.

For the longest time, she didn't sleep because
she was so scared he'd find her, and she knew if he
did, he'd end her life. He was a bully and thought
he could control her. For two years, she did
everything she could to stay away from his wrath.
People didn't understand how hard it was to get out
of an abusive relationship. Damned if you do and
damned if you don't. Her Aunt Evie begged her to
leave, but she didn't understand how hard it was to
go and be so scared that there were nights she'd lay
beside him wishing she had the courage to kill him.

She was so tired of looking over her shoulder,
expecting to see him. She never got a restraining
order against him because a piece of paper would
never stop him. Glancing at the clock, she saw it
was only nine, so she picked up her cellphone and
called her aunt.

"Hello, Piper," her aunt said when she answered.

"Hi, Aunt Evie. How are you and Uncle Drew
doing?"

"We're fine, honey. How about you?"

"I'm okay. I was wondering if Cory has been by?"

"Yes. I swear he's here once or twice a week since
you ran off. Drew is about ready to shoot his ass.
We won't tell him anything, sweetheart, you know
that."

"I know. It's just that...I'm so scared he'll find

me," she whispered.

"You should get in touch with the local police and let them know. In case he figures out where you are and heads there to look for you, they'll be on the lookout for him."

"I could do that, I guess." Piper nibbled on her lower lip, wondering if she should tell the police her problems and if it would even matter. "I've formed a friendship with the local vet, Dr. Tessa Garrett. Her husband is the sheriff here in Clifton. I could tell him."

"That would be a good idea, hon. Better safe than sorry. You should also get a dog. Most people hear a dog in someone's house; they won't enter."

"That's a great idea. I'll see if Stephanie minds if I get one, then go to the shelter after work on Monday if she says I can. I doubt the shelter is open on Sundays. I'm sure Tess, or even Sawyer, could help me with that."

"Who is Sawyer?" her aunt asked.

Who is Sawyer? Just the sexiest man she'd ever seen.

"Another vet, but he specializes in equine hydrotherapy. Frick is at his ranch now. It seems he may have arthritis in his knee."

"Who? Frick or Sawyer?" Her aunt chuckled.

Piper laughed. "Frick. I'm not sure Sawyer would appreciate me talking about him having arthritis."

"Being a man, probably not. They either have no aches and pains because they're too macho, or they have so many, they never shut up about them."

Her aunt always managed to make her laugh and forget her troubles. For a while, at least.

"I will look into getting a dog, though. I'll talk to Stephanie soon and ask." She yawned. "I'm sorry. I

42

am just so tired, and it's too early for bed."

"Honey, go to bed and get some rest. Knowing you, you don't sleep much. I'll let you know if he contacts us again, but Drew will have no problem telling him where to go, and it won't be to find you. I'm sure your parents won't tell him anything either. He'll probably head for Utah soon since he knows you're not here, thinking you're with your parents. Look at it this way, if he's still coming around here, then he's not close to finding you."

"That's true. I know Mom will call if he shows up."

"I'll call her tomorrow. I haven't talked to my sister in a while. Go to bed and try not to worry."

"All right. I love you both. Goodnight, Aunt Evie."

"We love you too, hon. Goodnight."

After plugging her cellphone into the charger, Piper pushed to her feet, stretched, then headed for the kitchen to make sure she had locked the door. Once she saw it was, she headed back through the living room, turning out lights as she did, and headed to her bedroom and into the attached bathroom to soak awhile before hitting the sheets.

She trembled as she thought of Cory finding her. A tear slid down her cheek because she knew he'd do all he could to make that happen. Monday, she'd go by to ask Tess about a dog and tell her about Cory. Piper had a feeling that Tess would want her to speak to Sam about it. Piper had never met the sheriff, but she could tell the community trusted him by how everyone talked about him.

After her bath, she crawled between the sheets, pulled them up to her chin, closed her eyes, and prayed for sleep to come.

****

Monday morning came too soon, Sawyer thought as he sat on the edge of the bed. Didn't he just go to bed?

"Shit," he muttered as he pushed to his feet and made his way to the bathroom to shave.

An hour later, with a cup of coffee in his hand, he made his way to his truck, climbed in then drove down to the barns. His home was about a half-mile from the office and barns. Once he took over the ranch, he had the new barns built away from the house. He didn't want clients coming to his home. They were to stop at the office. No one could go to the barns unless Peta called him and asked him. Then he'd send one of his workers to get them in a UTV. They kept the gates beside the office closed. Unless someone was bringing an animal to him, they remained that way. The barn close to the house was for his own horses.

As he pulled up to the barn, he glanced toward the office and saw Peta's little car pulling into a parking spot. She was so dependable. He had a good crew working for him. He watched as the door opened, and she stepped out and waved at him. He waved back, then entered the barn to see Trevor heading for him.

"Hey, boss. We tried to get Frick in the pool, but he refused, so we have him in one of the treadmills."

"Okay. Did he take to that all right?"

"Well, at first, he didn't like being boxed in, which is weird since he didn't mind the trailer, but once the water came in around him, he settled down. He seems to likc it now. He's been in there about ten minutes."

Sawyer slapped Trevor on the back. "Good. I'll be over in a while to check on him. I have some damn

44

paperwork to take care of first."

Trevor saluted, then jogged out of the barn to head back to the other one. Each horse would have three sessions of twenty minutes. Once their movements became regular and displayed no signs of stress, their owners could pick them up.

He headed for his office when his cellphone buzzed from his pocket. Stopping, he took it from the pocket to see the office number.

"What's up, Peta?"

"Marcia called for you again."

"Damn it. All right, I'll call her. Text her number to me."

He took a deep breath and entered his office, strode around the desk, and took a seat. His cellphone buzzed, and he saw the text from Peta with Marcia's number. He entered it into his phone. As it rang, he tried to figure out a way to get off the phone as soon as he could. What they had, ended a long time ago because she had screwed around on him.

"Hello?"

"Marcia, it's Sawyer."

"Why haven't you called me, Sawyer? I miss you," she purred in his ear.

"You can't possibly think I'm that stupid." He tried not to clench his teeth as he spoke.

"Well, I-I miss you. Can we get together? I can come there."

"Why? We're divorced. You liked screwing around too much." He ran a hand around the back of his neck. Damn, he hated this shit.

"I told you I was sorry," she snapped.

"And that means nothing to me," he growled out.

"It was a mistake...I'd like to try again," she

45

whispered.

"Let me put this in terms you'll understand...fuck no."

"People make mistakes, Sawyer."

"Yes, and mine was trusting you. I will never take you back."

"Never say never," she said in a quiet voice.

"Well, I'm saying it."

"We deserve a second chance. Don't you think so?"

"No, I don't."

"I am not giving up. You know how stubborn I can be. You loved me once, and no matter what you say, that love is still there. We have a daughter who would love to see her parents back together. See you soon." She hung up.

He looked at the phone in his hand and wondered what the hell had just happened. He had been faithful all the years they'd been married, but she had an affair. What she had done was unforgivable in his eyes. *See you soon?*

"What the fuck does that mean? Damn woman better not show up here." He had enough to deal with without coming here. It just came to him that she now had his new number. "Shit."

Shaking his head, he booted up the computer and got to work on the bills. It was going to be a long day.

****

After work, Piper walked through the parking lot to her SUV. The sweat ran down between her breasts and beaded above her upper lip. By the time she reached her vehicle, she felt sticky. She pointed the fob at her SUV to unlock it. When she opened the door, the heat poured out of it like an

46

oven when the door was ajar, and she had even cracked the windows. Who knew it would be this damn hot in Montana being so close to those majestic Glacier Mountains in the distance? But it was late in the summer and usually hot everywhere.

After she climbed in, she put the windows down once she started it to let some air circulate through. Lifting her hair off her nape, she fanned her hand to try to cool down.

Blowing out a breath, she put the gear into Drive and drove toward town. She had a few things to pick up, and she wanted to speak with Tess. Last night, she'd decided that talking with the sheriff about Cory was the smartest thing to do, but she also wanted Tess with her.

When she pulled into the animal hospital parking lot, she was a lot cooler. Pulling into a spot, she parked and stepped out. The heat, once again, slammed into her. Looking down at the hot blacktop, she saw little bubbles popping up. It was after five but still ridiculously hot.

Making her way to the glass doors, she pulled on one and entered the lobby, sighing as the colder air hit her hot skin.

"Hi, can I help you?"

Piper turned to see a pretty young woman behind the counter smiling at her.

"Hi. Yes, is Tess here?"

"Yes, is she expecting you?" The young woman with the name tag, *Jodi*, frowned up at her.

"No. I just wanted to talk to her for a minute, but if she's busy, I can call her later."

"Let me see," Jodi said as she picked up the phone. "What's your name?"

"Piper Howard. Thank you, Jodi."

She listened as Jodi spoke into the phone. Piper glanced around the lobby and thought it was a charming little place. She turned to look at Jodi when she heard her hang up the phone and smiled up at her.

"She'll be right out. She's on the phone with her husband right now."

"No problem." Piper smiled and leaned against the counter to wait.

A few minutes later, Tess entered the lobby with a smile on her face.

"Hi, Piper. Come on back to my office." She turned to lead the way.

They entered the office, and Tess closed the door, then motioned for Piper to take a seat.

"What can I do for you?"

"Well, two things. I wanted to ask you about adopting a dog," she said and nibbled on her lip. Sitting forward in the chair, she placed her arms on the desk.

"That's great. The shelter is full of them. From puppies to senior dogs. Do you know what you're looking for?"

"Well, I don't want a puppy, but if I get an adult dog, it will have to be house trained. I have to talk to Stephanie about it first, but I want one for...protection." She inhaled deeply. "I have an ex-boyfriend, who used to...beat me, and I know he's going to come looking for me," she said in a low tone of voice.

Tess hissed in a breath. "Have you told the police?"

"Not yet. That's the second thing. I want to, but if you could, I'd like you to be with me."

"That is no problem. Let me call Sam. He'll come over. He's in his office."

Piper watched as Tess picked up her cellphone and called the sheriff. She listened as Tess told Sam she needed him to come to her office, and no, nothing was wrong with her, but she needed him now. Then she hit *End* and placed the phone back on the desk.

"He'll be right here."

"Thank you," she whispered with embarrassment.

"Don't be embarrassed about this, Piper. It happens to a lot of women. We blame ourselves, but once we get away, we know we weren't the person in the wrong."

"*We?*"

"Yes, my first husband abused me. I was on the run from him and ended up here in Clifton. I met the love of my life while still married to that monster. I almost lost Sam over it because I didn't tell him I was still married while we were seeing each other. Even though I'd been in hiding for almost two years." Tess shrugged. "I was too scared to file for divorce for fear of *him* finding out where I was. I was so terrified he would find me, and he did."

"Oh, my God! What happened?"

"It's a long story, but he tried to kidnap me, and he shot one of Sam's deputies. Brody Morgan was with me, and Ryan shot him. When Sam came looking for us, he saw what was going on. Ryan was about to shoot Brody again when Sam shot through the doors in the lobby and killed that son of a bitch. I was finally free." She reached across the desk and touched Piper's hand. "I know what you're going through, and it is not your fault that he beat you.

49

Trust me on that."

A knock on the door startled Piper, and she glanced over her shoulder when the door opened, and a tall man entered. Piper widened her eyes and was sure her mouth dropped open because he was drop-dead gorgeous. His dark brown, almost black hair touched the collar of his khaki shirt, and he had the most amazing blue eyes. He smiled at her, giving her a nod, and strolled over to Tess, who stood to greet him with a kiss.

"Sam, this is Piper Howard, Piper, my husband, and the sheriff of Clifton County, Sam Garrett."

Piper stood and put her hand out to him. He had to be close to Sawyer and Bonner's height.

"Nice to meet you, Sheriff."

"Sam, please." He shook her hand then turned to Tess.

"What's going on, Tessa?"

"Take a seat, and we'll tell you," Tess said.

Sam frowned but nodded and waited for both women to sit before he did. He placed his ankle over the opposite knee, removed his cowboy hat, and hooked it on the toe of his boot.

She took a deep breath and told Sam about Cory. From the beginning of the beatings to her finally gaining the courage to sneak out in the middle of the night. She watched as Sam's jaw clenched and a muscle ticked in his cheek.

"I'm sorry you went through that. There's not much worse than a man who beats a woman, child, or animal. Are you sure he's coming here?"

"No, but it won't surprise me if he does. He won't give up trying to find me, and I'm afraid if he does, he won't stop until he kills me. I know I sound dramatic, but I know how mad he is that I left him."

50

Her voice caught, and Tess reached across the desk again to squeeze her hand.

"You do not sound dramatic. You're scared, and you know what he's capable of."

"I hope he doesn't show up at all, but it would be a bad time because there are a lot of tourists here now. I wouldn't be able to watch for him if he blends into the crowd." Sam frowned.

"I can try to get you a photo of him, but it will still be hard to spot him with all the people here," Piper whispered.

"A photo would be nice to go by, but I don't have a big department. Once the Bur Oak ranch and the Clifton Bed and Breakfast close, I'd have better luck spotting any strangers." Sam glanced at Tess. "I know when strangers are in my town. I'll also get with Grayson Beckett. He's the sheriff in Hartland County, and since that county surrounds Clifton, the towns of Clifton, Spring City, and Hartland will be covered."

"Well, I hope if he shows up, it's after the tourists leave. I'll see about finding a photo, but I left with only the clothes on my back, though."

"Do you know if he has a record?"

"I think he does. For assault of another woman, but it was years ago."

"Doesn't matter how long ago it was. What's his last name?"

Piper gave him Cory's full name and watched as Sam wrote it down, then stuck the paper in the pocket of his khaki shirt.

"I'll look him up."

"Okay, I appreciate it. Both of you are wonderful to help me." She told Sam and Tess.

"It's how these little towns are. We're family. I

found that out when I moved here and had trouble when Ryan showed up," Tess said.

Sam took his hat from his boot, placed it on his head, and stood. "I don't like trouble in my county, and I know Gray is the same way, so we'll keep a lookout for him, and if he shows up, it'll be taken care of."

"Thank you, Sam." Piper stood and held her hand out to him, which he took.

"I'll see you at home, angel," he said as he looked at Tess, touched the brim of his hat, and left the office. His boot heels clacked down the hallway as he headed for the lobby, then she heard him say goodbye to Jodi.

"Tess, he's a great guy. Not to mention gorgeous. I can see how you fell for him," Piper said with a grin.

"I fell for him the minute I looked up at him, but I kept telling myself I couldn't get involved. A lot of good that did me." Tess laughed.

"I appreciate you both."

"It's what friends do. After you find out from Stephanie about having a dog, we can go to the shelter together, if you'd like."

"I'd love it. I'm going to head to the diner for dinner since I'm in town, and I'll talk to her once I get home."

"Great. I have a feeling she'll let you have a dog. She is such a nice person, plus the fact that when Bonner lived in that house, he had a dog." Tess stood. "Have a good evening, and try not to worry about Cory. I doubt he's found you."

"My Aunt Evie said he's been to their place, and as long as he's there, I'm safe, but I know he will not give up on finding me."

"Sam will do all he can to protect you if he does. Get your dinner. I'm about to close, and I know Jodi's ready to go."

"Have a good evening. I'll get back to you after I talk with Stephanie."

"Sounds good. Call me. Goodnight."

Piper waved, turned, and made her way down the hallway. She said goodbye to Jodi, walked outside and into the suffering heat again.

After climbing into her vehicle, she headed for the diner. Those burgers seemed to be calling her name.

After finding a spot in the diner parking lot, she stepped from her SUV and moaned at the smell coming from the little restaurant. It looked crowded, so she hoped she could find a place to sit. She'd sit at the counter if she had to.

Opening the door, the bell above it jingled, announcing her presence. People waved and called out to her. She smiled and gave a wave. This little town was so friendly. She loved it here and had no desire to leave. She hoped that never happened. It depended on if Cory found her.

Sighing, she let her eyes roam the restaurant and saw a few empty seats at the counter. She took a seat and picked up the menu. She loved the burgers, so she wasn't sure why she was even looking.

"Is this seat taken?" a deep voice asked her, and she looked up to see Sawyer standing beside the empty stool.

"Nope. Have a seat." She smiled at him.

Sawyer nodded and took the empty stool.

"How are you today?" he asked her.

"Good. You?"

"Same. Frick's doing well. He liked the water treadmill but hated the pool, so we're going to keep him using the treadmill."

"I'm glad he's doing so well. His brother misses him."

"Hi, Sawyer. Piper."

Piper looked up to see Deidra Mitchell smiling at her.

"Hello, Deidra. How are you?" Piper asked.

"Being run ragged. What can I get you two?"

"My usual is fine," Sawyer said.

"Since I don't have a usual yet, I'll take a cheeseburger with onion, lettuce, tomato, and mustard."

"Got it. It will be right up."

"Deidra? How's Preston? I haven't seen him in a while."

"He's just fine, Sawyer. He should be here in a few minutes to pick me up."

"Good. I'd love to say hello to him."

The bell over the door rang.

"There he is now. I'll get your orders to Uncle Owen, and Rissa will bring them to you. Enjoy." Deidra smiled, moved around the counter, and walked to the tall man who had entered.

Piper couldn't take her eyes off the man. He was very good-looking. Tall, with black hair, he shook hands with just about everyone. She saw him grin when he spotted Deidra. Everyone whooped and hollered when he pulled her to him, lifted her, and took her lips in a deep kiss. Piper laughed.

"I bet Deidra's face is beet red," she said.

"No doubt there. They recently got married. Preston is crazy about her, and the feeling is mutual."

"He's sexy." Piper laughed when Sawyer spun around on the stool to face her.

"He is, huh?"

"Yep, though not as sexy as a certain veterinarian."

Sawyer's eyebrows shot up. "Tess?"

Piper burst out laughing. "Yeah, Tess."

Sawyer chuckled. "Don't tell Sam."

"I won't. How was your day?"

"Tiring, but I love it. So, when will you make dinner for me?"

She watched as his eyes dropped to her lips, then back to her eyes, and she suppressed a shiver. She was not used to a man looking at her the way he did.

"How about Saturday night at six?"

"Not sooner?"

"No, some nights I work over, and I'm too tired even to think, let alone cook."

"You never said what you do."

"I'm a hospital administrator at Clifton Memorial."

"What is that, exactly?"

"It's a hospital in Clifton." She laughed when he narrowed his eyes at her. "I'm responsible for managing the financial budget, which includes spending accounts and rates for services. Hiring, scheduling staff members, and working with the board of directors."

"Did you have Friday off?"

"Yes. I took a few days off."

"How did you get a job like that here?"

"I told you I'd been at Bur Oak, and on one excursion to town, I fell in love with Clifton. Willa Callahan told me they only took guests to Spring

City, but she had convinced Devin and Jaxon to add Clifton and Hartland. Once I walked down the sidewalks here, I fell in love. When I got back to Wyoming, I sent a resume to the hospital here. Finally, they sent me a letter saying that they wanted to hire me. They had given me two weeks to start the job, and I almost called them back to tell them I couldn't make it. The night I left Cory, I had four days to get here. Aunt Evie and Uncle Drew made it happen."

"Are you going to tell me what happened between you and him?"

"Maybe on Saturday. It's not a pretty story, but I want you to know about it. I don't want secrets between us."

"I don't either, so we'll have a nice talk at dinner."

"Here you go. Enjoy your dinners," Rissa Maddox said as she set their plates down in front of them, then walked off.

Piper looked at Sawyer and grinned when he winked at her. She picked up her burger. She couldn't wait for Saturday.

Chapter Three

Saturday evening at six, Sawyer pulled into the driveway of the small cabin where Piper lived. Throwing the gear into Park, he picked up the flowers on the passenger seat, exited the vehicle, and made his way to the door. He knocked on it, and when it opened, he about dropped to his knees. God, she was beautiful. Her T-shirt and jeans hugged her body, and on her feet were white flip-flops. He grinned when he saw the pink toenails.

"Hi," he said, smiling.

"Hi yourself. Come on in." She opened the door wider, and he walked across the threshold.

"Something smells great."

"Pot roast. I hope you like it."

"Pot roast is one of my favorites. These are for you." He held the flowers out to her.

"They're beautiful, thank you," she whispered and lowered her face into them.

Frowning, Sawyer tipped her chin up with his finger.

"I didn't get them to make you cry." He shrugged. "They're just flowers."

"No one has ever given me flowers."

"Damn it," he muttered and pulled her into his arms.

Her arms wrapped around his waist, and she put her face against his neck. Damn, it felt fantastic holding her.

After a few minutes, she pulled away from him and looked up at him. Tears spiked her lashes, and he couldn't stop himself from kissing her for all the money in the world. But he lowered his head slowly in case she didn't want him to. He cupped her face in his hands, and his lips touched hers, and a shock ran through him. When she moaned, he wanted to back her against the wall and fuck her senseless. No woman had ever affected him this much, this fast. He deepened the kiss and moved his tongue into her mouth and her arms wrapped around his neck. He slowly lifted his lips from hers and put his forehead against hers.

She stared up at him, nibbled on her bottom lip, then a slow smile lifted her lips.

"Maybe you should bring me flowers more often."

He blew out a laugh. "If I get that kind of reaction, I'll bring them every time, and I want there to be more times, Piper. I hope you do too."

Reaching up, she removed his cowboy hat, tossed it on a bench sitting beside the door, and ran her fingers through his hair.

"Oh, I do, cowboy. I definitely do."

Leaning down, he gave her a quick kiss and grinned.

"Thank God."

She ran the tip of her finger over his mustache. "It tickles."

Sawyer raised his eyebrows. "Do you want me to shave it off?"

Piper looked shocked. "You'd do that?"

He shrugged. "I would. Especially if we're going to continue to see each other. If you don't like it—"

"I do like it. Don't shave it off. Let me put these in water. They're so pretty." She moved away from him and moved to a cupboard.

"Just wildflowers. I saw them on the way here and stopped to pick them-what?"

"You picked them?" she said as she spun around to look at him.

"Was that wrong of me?"

She walked to him, wrapped her arms around his waist, and kissed his cheek. He wasn't sure how it could be wrong, but women think way too differently than men. She stepped out of his arms, and he watched as she put the flowers in a vase, filled it with water, and set it on the table.

"No, it wasn't wrong at all. Few men will take the time to pick wildflowers. At least, none that I know. Let me get dinner, then we can sit in the living room and get to know each other."

"Sounds good, darlin'." He pulled a kitchen chair out with his booted foot and took a seat.

"You can go in the living room."

"Nah, I'm fine right here. Watching you." He chuckled when she blushed.

After dinner, which he told her was great, they made their way to the living room with coffee. She took a seat on the sofa, and he sat down beside her. He lightly touched her hair.

"So soft," he murmured.

"Tell me about you, Sawyer. How did you get into equine hydrotherapy?"

"I was in college working on my degree when I heard about it and decided that was what I wanted to add to my practice."

"The one in Bozeman?"

"Yes, ma'am. Right after I graduated, I was hired at an animal hospital in Bozeman. I worked there for about a year before deciding to purchase my own place. I did okay, but once I added the hydrotherapy, the practice took off. I still own the hospital in Bozeman."

"What degree do you need for that?" She sipped her coffee, and he had a hell of a time keeping his eyes off her lips as they caressed the cup.

"Uh, I have a certificate in equine rehabilitation, which means I'm a Certified Equine Rehabilitation Practitioner."

"How long did that take?"

Shit! She needed to quit putting her lips on the rim of that cup because he was feeling them on his...get your fucking mind out of the gutter, Griffin.

"About six months, depending on how much time you can spend doing it. Since it's for practicing vets, it can stretch out longer."

"You spent a lot of time on education."

"I did. I came back to Clifton because Dad couldn't work on the ranch anymore. He has bad knees, so he moved to Arizona about four years ago. I took over the ranch and turned it into what it is today with Dad's blessing since the ranch is still his. I helped Tess out for a while, but this is what I wanted to do full time. Since Doc Carter retired a few years back, he hasn't been able to help at the hospital any longer, so when Tess and Sam go on vacations, or she takes a day off, I fill in for her."

****

"Doc Carter?" Piper frowned since she'd never heard of him.

"He owned the Clifton Animal Hospital before Tess did. When he retired, he offered to sell it to her, and she bought it. She's a hell of a vet."

"You are, too, if she refers people to you. Tell me about your marriage."

Sawyer raked his fingers through his hair.

"Marcia and I were college sweethearts. I wanted to wait to get married, but she talked me into it

60

when we were nineteen, and we got married a year later. She loved living in Bozeman, and we were happy. She got pregnant right away, and I loved the idea of having kids. When Brooke came along, I was ecstatic. But Marcia didn't seem to enjoy motherhood. I mean, don't get me wrong, she was a good mom, but she'd rather be out spending my money. I spoiled both of them. I could afford it." He shrugged. "Everything was fine until Dad decided to move to Arizona, and I wanted to return here. Marcia wasn't happy at all. She hated this one-church town, as she called it. She hated being alone, she said. All I did was work on getting the ranch up and running with the hydrotherapy, and I'd go to seminars about it a good bit. Brooke had stayed in Bozeman with Marcia's sister, so she could finish high school there then go to the university in Oregon."

"So what happened with Marcia? You were married a long time."

"Yeah, we were. It just all fell apart when we moved here, and she screwed around on me."

"Oh, wow. How did you find out?"

"She told me—"

"She *told* you?" Piper thought the woman had balls, that was for sure.

"Yes. I was gone for a convention, and when I got home, she said she had to confess something then told me she'd been having an affair. I sure never expected that. I made her leave, and I divorced her. Of course, it was all *my* fault."

"How was that your fault?"

"I was gone all the time. I spent too much time working, all that shit, but yet, she loved the money I made. I was still going to seminars, and she said

61

she got lonely."

"That's not an excuse."

"I agree. It hurt, I won't lie, but damn it, I believe in those wedding vows." He shrugged. "She didn't."

"Do you have any siblings?"

"I have a younger brother. What about you?"

"No, I'm an only child. Tell me about your brother."

"Colson is five years younger than me. We haven't talked in years."

"Why not?"

Sawyer huffed out a laugh. "We used to get along great when we were kids. He was my baby brother." He shook his head. "But he got in with a dangerous crowd when he was only twelve, and they were nothing but trouble, and he stayed in trouble until he was sixteen. He was arrested for stealing a car when he was just thirteen. The cops brought him to the house to see what Dad wanted to do with him since they knew Dad, and they didn't want to take Colson to juvie without talking to him first. I was so angry with him that I told Dad the best thing to do with him *was* to put him in juvenile detention because he'd just keep getting into trouble. I knew by the look on Colson's face that he never expected me to suggest that. He and that bunch broke into cars, took them for joy rides, and then it escalated to breaking into businesses. Who knew how it could have worsened? Even the cops said he was on a dangerous path. Well, Dad agreed that something drastic needed to be done, so he told the cops to take him away. It pissed me off that Colson did the shit he did. He hit me that night. He was only thirteen, but he stood up to me, and when he threw that punch, it took all I had not to hit him back, but he was just a kid." Sawyer sighed. "He spent the night in juvie, then the next morning, he was taken to see a judge and sent home on probation. I guess because it was his first offense. So he thought he could do whatever he wanted. He went right back to doing what put him in there, and he'd end up back in juvenile detention. He was nothing but trouble for Dad, and he didn't care. I know how upset he was when Mom died, but he should have had enough of juvie to not want to go back, but anytime he got caught, they'd send him back. It didn't seem to bother him. The last time he got arrested, I came home from college and jumped all over him. Dad told Colson that if he didn't straighten up, he'd kick him off the ranch." Sawyer blew out a humorless laugh. "It didn't bother him. He ran away, and that about killed Dad. He was a damn hellion. He didn't care about anyone but himself. The police picked him up and, once again, sent him to juvie, and this time they sentenced him. He made Dad's life miserable for three years. When he was sixteen, he was arrested for possession of marijuana. I'd had it with him by then. We never spoke after that, and Dad was never happy about it. I think Colson's lawyer put the fear of God in him. He told him that prison was a hell of a lot worse, and if he didn't straighten up, that was where he was headed. I think if he had straightened up after the first time, we'd be fine. I could forgive and forget one time, but he didn't stop at once. He just kept getting into trouble."

"Did he still talk to your dad?"

"After a while, yes, but never me."

"Don't you think it's past time to work it out? I can tell you're still hurt by it."

63

"Colson and I will probably never speak to each other again."

"Where is he? Do you know?"

Sawyer smirked. "He lives in Kalispell. He's a vet, like Dad and me. When we were boys, we talked about working together one day. That will never happen. After he graduated from high school, he attended vet school like I did. I know he'd visit Dad when he knew I wouldn't be there, but we haven't seen each other in years."

"How many?"

"Damn, probably five, and we had another argument then. I told him to get the hell away from me and stay away."

"Why did you argue? Never mind, it's none of my business."

"It's fine, just the same old, same old. Dad wanted us both home for Thanksgiving one year, and Colson was talking with Dad about his practice, and I said it was a wonder he even made it out of high school." Sawyer shook his head. "I know he blames me for him being arrested. Which is true. I was just so damn disappointed in him because he knew better. Dad did everything for both of us, and Colson was a damn juvenile delinquent. I could understand if Dad mistreated him, but he didn't. He's a great father, and I was angry that Colson hurt him like that. All we ever did since the first time he was arrested was argue. We could never be in the same room without getting into it."

"Well, apparently, he turned his life around."

"Yes, and Dad is so proud of him, but he's still upset that we don't speak."

"Aren't you proud of him? He followed in his big

brother's footsteps."

"He followed in *Dad's* footsteps. It's like I'm waiting for him to mess up again. He's thirty-eight, and Dad says he's doing great, but I feel like the other shoe's going to drop. He could be past all of that, but I saw firsthand how he didn't give a damn about anyone but himself. We will never be close again."

"It's because he was in trouble when he was younger, and it's hard for you to get past that. People change, Sawyer."

"Some do. It tore Dad up. He blamed himself, but it was no one's fault but Colson's. Like I said, the last time we saw each other, we got into a fight."

"Fistfight?"

"Yeah, I think I'd been waiting for the opportunity to hit him back all those years."

"Men," Piper said and shook her head. "Did you get the better of him?"

"It was about even. He's the same height and build I am. Dad broke us up, and that's when I told Colson to stay away from me. Brooke adored him, so it hurt her when he left. She blamed me for it."

"I didn't know you could get into college with a record."

"Sure you can. Many colleges have that question on the application, but it doesn't mean you won't get in. Besides, after Colson decided to straighten up, the good grades in high school got him in. His juvie records were sealed once he turned eighteen, but he had to be honest on the application."

"I'm sorry you don't speak with him, though. Does your dad like living in Arizona?"

"Yes. He seems to love the warmer climate there. Oh, and back to Marcia. She called me the other day. Said she wanted to work it out. I told her no way in hell. Last I heard, she had gotten married, but it only lasted two years. She probably screwed around on him too."

"I can't believe she would think you'd be willing to work it out if she slept with another man."

"Yeah, that will not happen. It made me wonder if that had been the first time she did it to me. Tell me about you, Piper," he said.

"I have a bachelor's degree in healthcare practice management."

"Tell me about the man you were with for two years."

She took a deep breath. This wasn't going to be easy, but she would not lie about Cory and how he treated her.

"I met Cory through a mutual friend three years ago, and we started dating. He was charming, attentive, and good to me...until we moved in together. His jealousy made us fight constantly. I don't know why he acted the way he did. I never gave him any reason. The first time he hit me—"

"What?" Sawyer growled out in a low tone of voice.

"Yes, I was a victim of domestic abuse. Being with a man still scares me, but I know not all men are like that—"

"We sure as shit aren't."

"I know. The first time he hit me was during an argument. I immediately packed my clothes to leave, but he beat me so severely that my eyes were swollen shut, and he swore I would never walk away from him. I should have gone anyway, but I was scared. So very scared. Then it happened again and again. The worst beating I got was after I'd been out with friends for one of their birthdays. He accused me of flirting with every man in the bar, and it was stupid for someone as bad as I was in bed to flirt with any man. Then when he said I wasn't *allowed* to go out without him, I laughed. I was a little drunk, or trust me, I never would have laughed. He knocked me to the floor and beat the hell out of me. Just like he had threatened to do anytime I talked about leaving. He scared me so much. The night I got away, he choked me until I passed out. He had a fit when I let him run out of beer—"

"*You* let him run out of beer? Couldn't he get it himself?"

"You'd think so, wouldn't you? I really meant to get some because I knew he'd be angry." She shook her head. "What an understatement. I woke up at two in the morning, and he was asleep. I got out of bed, out of the house, and to my car, then drove to my aunt and uncle's place. The entire time, I was sure he was on my tail, and if he got a hold of me, he would kill me for sure. I was too scared to do anything. I thought if I pressed charges and they didn't stick, he'd kill me. I lived in constant fear. Hell, I still do." Her breath hitched, and Sawyer wrapped his arms around her.

"I'm glad you got away from him. But I'd like to kick his ass."

"Looking back now, I know it was wrong to stay, but each time the beatings would get worse. I can't tell you how many times he'd push me against a wall and tell me he'd kill me if I ever left him. I never thought I would be the type of woman to put up with that, but I honestly know why women don't leave abusive men."

"Unbelievable."

"My aunt told me he showed up at their place, but they wouldn't tell him anything. Cory will go to Utah, where my parents live. I know my Uncle Drew told him to get the hell off his property, but it worries me what Cory will do to find me. My father is very religious, but I've heard him swear anytime Cory's name was mentioned. My parents don't know about him hitting me, and even my aunt and uncle don't know the full extent of it."

"I think I like your dad and uncle."

"They're wonderful men." She pushed to her feet and looked down at Sawyer. "Give me your cup, and I'll take them to the kitchen. Would you like some dessert?"

A slow grin lifted his lips. "Depends on what or who it is."

Piper laughed. "Hold that thought. I'll be right back."

"Yes, ma'am."

She wasn't sure what made her do it, but she leaned down and softly kissed his lips.

"We'll talk about dessert." She laughed when he groaned, then she walked out of the room.

Once in the kitchen, she leaned against the counter and took a deep breath. The man was just too sexy and gorgeous for her peace of mind. But she had never felt like this about a man. She put the cups in the sink after rinsing them and headed back to the living room. He sat on the sofa with his head back and his eyes closed. When she took a seat beside him, his eyes opened, and he raised his head, looked at her, and she swore her heart stopped.

"You talk about your aunt and uncle a good bit.

Aren't you close to your parents?"

"I am. They're just very controlling. I moved in with Cory against their wishes. Seems I should have listened to them. My aunt is my mother's sister. Night and day. I spent more time with Aunt Evie than I did with Mom. Evie is such a character, and Uncle Drew is the same. I love them."

"Sounds like they love you too."

"They do, and I know that with all my heart. I was engaged when I was twenty-eight, but he liked other women too much. I have little luck with men."

"Maybe that will change," he murmured.

"Maybe it will," she whispered. "Do you want to get married?"

His eyebrows shot up. "You asking?"

"No! Just curious."

Sawyer blew out a laugh.

"I'd like to get married again, but I'm wary. I want to trust the woman I marry."

"Glad you're smart about it." She tilted her head.

"So, tell me how you ended up with horses if your ex didn't want to let you out of his sight. I would think he wouldn't want you going anywhere to ride."

"Aunt Evie introduced me to riding when I was a little girl. They own a ranch. She and Uncle Drew bought both of my horses for me. Since Frick was an older horse, they got him cheap, and they took him and Frack from the same farmer who was abusing them. It took me a while to get the horses to trust me. That was about the only place I was...*allowed* to go without Cory, but I had to be home by a certain time, and I would be, just to keep him from getting angry."

"Ass. I'm glad you got the horses to trust you.

They can be uneasy, but they have great instincts about people. If treated right, they're faithful companions."

"I know that's right. Frick tried to bite Cory." She laughed.

Sawyer chuckled. "Just like dogs. They know who's a good person and who isn't."

Piper stared at him and knew that Sawyer Griffin was a good man.

"Do you live on the ranch?" She frowned. "I didn't see a house."

"It sits back in the woods. There's a road leading from the barns to the house. My father inherited the house from his father. It's been handed down through generations to the oldest child. When my father passes away, I'll inherit it. There's a barn close to it I keep my horses in. I added the other barns for the therapy."

"What about Colson? What will he inherit?"

"I'm sure he'll be left money. It's the way it's always been in the Griffin family."

"You mentioned your mother passed away. Tell me about her," she said.

"She passed away when I was sixteen. She was a wonderful woman who loved her sons. I think if she had lived, Colson wouldn't have turned to crime. She adored him. Oh, I know she loved me too, but he was her baby. He took it damn hard. Dad raised us, and I know Dad still misses her. I think that's one reason he moved away from the ranch."

"It's an impressive operation you have there."

"It keeps me busy." Sawyer pushed to his feet. "I'd better get going. I have an early morning."

"You work on Sundays?"

"Sweetheart, I work every day. The practice isn't open, but I still have to work in my barns and on some patients. Come on," he said as he put his hand out to her. She placed her hand in his, and he pulled her to her feet. He cupped her face in his hands, leaned down to kiss her. When she wrapped her arms around his waist, he deepened the kiss, then slowly raised his head. "Want to take that bet yet?"

Laughing, she shook her head. "Not ready for that yet. I'm not sure I'd ever be ready for you."

"Why not?"

"I'm a lousy lay, remember?"

"I don't believe that for a second. That jackass wasn't doing his job. He was only in it for himself."

"Probably."

"No probably about it. Another bet you want to take?"

"Nope. You're too confident."

"You think so? I'm forty-three years old, Piper. I know what to do with a woman." He kissed her forehead. "I have to go. Walk me out."

She took his hand, led him from the living room to the kitchen, and watched as he took his hat off the bench, placed it on his head, and tugged the brim down low. Damn. She didn't know if she liked him more with it on or off.

"Be careful going home. Thank you for the flowers."

"Thank you for dinner. It was great. Maybe I'll cook the next time."

"I'd love that." She stood on her toes and quickly kissed his lips. "Goodnight."

"Goodnight, baby. Sleep well." He tapped the brim of his hat, turned, and walked out the door.

71

Piper waited until she heard his truck start and drive away before turning off the porch light and locking the door. She made her way to the bathroom to take a bath to relax. All the talk about Cory had made her tense. As she walked down the hallway, though, she couldn't keep the smile from her face.

****

The following week, Sawyer stood at one pool and watched as Trevor and Brick led the horse around, making it swim against the current. This horse was a regular, and Sawyer was at the point where he believed the horse acted lame so he could swim in the pool since he seemed to enjoy it so much.

"He likes this way too much," Brick said with a laugh.

"I think he fakes it so he can come here. Look at him. I bet you could let go of the ropes, and he'd swim on his own." Sawyer shook his head.

His cellphone buzzed, and he picked it up to see the office number.

"What's up, Peta?" Sawyer said as he answered.

"Marcia is here," she said in a low voice, and he knew it was because she didn't want Marcia to hear her.

"What the hell is she doing here?"

"She said she wants to see you, so you need to get up here. Her words, not mine."

"Damn it. All right, tell her I'll be there in a few minutes." Sawyer hit *End* on his phone and swore under his breath. Why the hell was she back?

"Everything okay, Doc?" Brick asked him.

"Yes. No. Marcia's here. I'll be back in a few minutes."

72

"Good luck with that," Brick said with a laugh. Sawyer raised his middle finger at him as he left the barn.

He climbed into one of the UTVs, started it, and drove to the office. All the while wondering what the hell she was doing here.

"Well, she did tell you she'd see you soon. Son of a bitch," he muttered.

After he reached the office, he parked, walked up the steps, and entered the building. He turned to see Marcia sitting on the bench inside the door. She was still a beautiful woman. She was tall, almost five foot nine, with an impressive figure and perfectly styled red hair, and yet she did nothing for him anymore. She stood when she saw him, smiled, walked to him, and tried to put her arms around him, but he stepped away from her.

"What are you doing here, Marcia?"

"I told you I'd see you soon. Can we go somewhere and talk?" She glanced at Peta, then back at him.

Sawyer looked at Peta to see her frowning and flattening her lips. Not a good sign. He took Marcia's arm in his hand, walked outside, and stopped on the porch.

"There is nothing to talk about. I said everything I needed to say in our last conversation."

"It's too hot out here, Sawyer. Let's go somewhere cooler."

Sawyer stared at her and frowned. Did she not hear what he just said?

"No. Go home. I have work to do." He started down the steps, but her voice stopped him.

"As usual. This is what broke us up. You cared more about those filthy animals than you did about me. *Us*," she snapped.

He spun around, stormed back up the steps, and advanced toward her, making her back up.

"First off, there is no *us*. Second, this is my *job*. I'm a *veterinarian*. As you call them, those filthy animals and their owners depend on me, and this isn't what broke us up. You broke it up by fucking around. What the fuck do we need to discuss?" he said through clenched teeth.

Her eyes widened as she backed into the building. Her bottom lip quivered. But he knew it was all an act. She had perfected that years ago, and he wasn't falling for it ever again.

"And if you would have been home more, it never would have happened."

"Bullshit, Marcia. Just leave, and do not come back."

"I have told you over and over that I'm sorry," she snapped.

"And I've told you I don't care. I'm seeing someone else now, anyway. Get the hell off my property." He practically ran down the steps and climbed into the UTV. After starting it, he tore out of the parking lot, throwing gravel and dust in his wake.

"Seeing someone else? You had one date, and that was dinner at her place," he said as he headed for the barn.

Removing his cellphone from his T-shirt pocket, he called Piper but hung up because she was probably busy at work. He was putting it back into his pocket when it buzzed. He grinned when he saw her name.

"Hey," he said.

"Why did you hang up?"

"I just realized that you were probably busy at work, and I didn't want to bother you."

"I am at work, but not busy right now. I'm all alone in my office."

"Too bad I can't visit. Would you like to go to dinner on Friday night? I can make reservations at Hartland Restaurant."

"I have plans for Friday night, but what about Saturday?"

"Plans?" He hoped it wasn't a date with another man, but they never discussed not seeing anyone else. Hell, they never discussed seeing each other.

"Yep. I am going out with the girls. I can't wait. Tess invited me. She said they all get together once a month."

Sawyer chuckled. "Yeah, I've heard of those once a month things with that bunch. Okay, I'll call and make reservations for Saturday around seven. Sound good?"

"It does. I'll see you then. Have a good day."

"You too, darlin'." He hit *End* and put the phone back into his pocket, and continued to the barn. The day just got better.

****

Friday night, Piper sat at a table in the local bar and laughed so much her cheeks hurt. Tess had introduced her to the women, and all of them seemed close.

"I forgot to mention that I met Willa and Presley when I stayed at the Bur Oak ranch a year ago. It was one time I stood up to Cory." Piper's voice shook, and she cleared her throat. As she glanced around the table, she kept her voice low.

"He beat you when you got back, didn't he?" Tess whispered.

75

"Yes, and that was when I sent a resume here to the hospital. I fell in love with the area when I visited it on a trip to town with some Bur Oak guests. I knew I had to get away from him. I was so happy when the hospital sent me a letter and offered me the job. They had fired me from the hospital I worked at in Casper because I missed too much work. They didn't know it was because my face was bruised and swollen." She shook her head. "I almost didn't make it here, but it was my time to get away from him."

"Don't worry, we'll keep an eye out. I promise. When Ryan came here after me, he terrified me because I knew what he was capable of, and he was so angry with me for running away. It took him two years to find me, so by then, he was royally pissed. If you ever need to talk, call me, or come see me. I know what you're going through." Tess took a deep breath and blew it out. "Those of us who go through anything like that have scars for life. Kelsey's husband, Ryder, and Katie's husband, Riley, were both beaten as children. They have scars too, but with Kelsey's and Katie's love, they've put it behind them. Riley's father was horrible. Ryder's wasn't much better, but they're loved now, and they know it. Just like I know Sam loves me, and he would never raise a hand to me. Not all men are like that."

"I know. I'm just scared Cory is going to find me. He won't give up, Tess."

"I know because Ryan didn't either. We'll keep an eye out. We should tell the others. Especially Becca because she owns the B and B. She can tell Evelyn, the cook, and the women at the front desk to let her know if any new guests arrive matching Cory's description."

"That's a good idea. Maybe I could talk to Willa or Presley about it too."

"Yep. Sam could give motels a photo of him too. That way, we've got every place covered. Sam already told Gray about it and gave him photos to distribute in his county."

"Good. Hopefully, that will cover all the bases." Piper smiled at her new friend.

Tess smiled, then she frowned as she looked at something over Piper's shoulder. Piper turned to see a cowboy heading for the table, swaying as he did. Piper looked back to Tess to see her shake her head, and the cowboy turned and made his way back through the crowd. The women laughed and ordered more drinks.

"Hello, ladies."

Piper looked up to see a beautiful redhead. She had a tray against her hip as she smiled at the women. Tess jumped up, hugged her, and turned to Piper.

"Piper, this is Scarlett Robinson, Scarlett, meet Piper Howard."

"Nice to meet you, Piper. I hope you're enjoying yourself."

"I am, thank you, Scarlett. It's nice to meet you too."

"Do y'all need any refills?" The women shook their heads. "All right. Let me know if you do. I don't want any of my customers unhappy." Scarlett smiled, then walked back to the bar.

"She is gorgeous and seems so nice," Piper said.

"Scarlett is a wonderful person. She just recently moved here. Her uncle owns the bar, but she's going to buy it. Dewey wants to retire. We all love her already," Tess said.

Later, they all made their way back to the table after a few line dances. Piper was sure she would be sore tomorrow from working muscles she hadn't used in a while. She hoped they invited her every month because she needed this. She needed to go home and not worry about being beaten for staying out or flirting with every guy in the place. Something she never did, but it hadn't mattered to Cory.

As she glanced around, she smiled. Dewey's was a typical cowboy bar. Jeans, T-shirts, cowboy hats, and boots were everywhere. The music was loud, but the band was great. For the first time since being with Cory, she knew she didn't have to worry about going home to him.

"I can't believe it's almost midnight," Liv Stone said from across the table.

"Do you have a curfew?" Tess asked her.

"Nope, but I want to get home before Wyatt goes to sleep," Liv said with a smile.

"Oh, dear Lord, Liv. I don't know how that man can stand up. You never let him rest," Emma Stone said with a laugh.

"I love my husband, and as I've said a million times, he's great in bed." Liv shrugged.

"We all think our men are great in bed, or we wouldn't be with them, but we let them get some rest," Katie Madison said.

Madilyn Morgan snorted. "I can't keep my hands off Brody. Poor man."

"See? It ain't just me," Liv said as she folded her arms and smirked.

"I haven't had sex in so long I'm not sure I remember how to do it," Piper muttered. "And the last time I had sex, it was so bad. I think I fell asleep."

The women burst out laughing.

"Then you need to find a good man." Stephanie smiled at her. "Come to think of it, you took your horse to Sawyer..."

"That's right, you did," Tess said. "Now that man is hot."

Piper looked around the table, and all of them were nodding their heads. She gave them a big grin.

"I'm having dinner with him tomorrow night." She told them about the bet, which made them all laugh, and they suggested she take it.

"I bet you lose," Liv said, laughing.

"God, I sure hope I do," Piper said, making them howl with laughter.

"I think we need to get going. It is getting late, and all this sex talk wants me to make sure Stone is awake when I get home." Becca grinned.

Piper thought it was funny that Becca called her husband Jake by his last name. She'd explained she had since day one, and it stuck, just like him calling her Red. Yep, Piper loved these women already and knew she'd made some new friends. She knew she could depend on them. She knew they'd be there for her if she needed them. After telling them about Cory, she did not doubt that these women had her back. For that, she was thankful.

Everyone stood to leave, then walked outside. The heat from the day still lingered, even though it was after midnight. They hugged each other, got in their vehicles, and headed home with promises to get together for lunch one day at the diner.

Piper smiled the entire ride home as Becca, Tess, Emma, and Liv talked about their husbands. She couldn't wait to see Sawyer tomorrow night. She just might take that bet.

Chapter Four

Sawyer pulled up to the little house, parked, and stepped out into the heat. Damn, it was hot. Summer was a real bitch this year. Hell would probably be cooler, he thought with a grin.

Shoving the door closed, he walked up the steps and knocked on the door. It opened, and his breath whooshed out of his body as he looked at her. Her beautiful hair was down, touching her shoulders, and the blue dress she wore emphasized every curve. His eyes skimmed down, and he swallowed hard as he looked at the skimpy heels on her feet. They were white, with a thin strap across her toes and one around her ankles. The heel was high, putting her close to six-two. *Son of a bitch.* His dick twitched just looking at those shoes and thinking of them hooked behind his back. When she cleared her throat, he raised his eyes to stare into hers.

"I really wish you'd take that bet," he murmured as he leaned down to give her a quick kiss.

Piper laughed. "We'll see."

"You look amazing."

"Thank you. I wasn't sure what to wear because I didn't know what kind of restaurant it was. I called Tess and asked her." She shrugged. "I haven't worn heels this high in forever."

"Well, wear them more often."

"Maybe I will if we go out again."

"*If?* Oh, darlin', we are definitely going out again." He put his hand out to her. "Let's go before I change my mind and try to talk you into taking that bet."

She laughed as she placed her hand in his. After she locked the door, he led her to the passenger side of his truck, opened the door, and helped her in. *Holy shit!* That dress was going to drive him insane. And he refused to look down at her feet. He slammed the door a little harder than he'd intended and strode around the front to his side. He tugged the door open, slid onto the seat, took a deep breath, and inserted the key to start the truck. When she snorted, he glanced over to her.

"Are you upset about something, Sawyer?" she asked him with the innocence of a whore in church.

"You wore those damn shoes to kill me, didn't you?"

When she burst out laughing, he shook his head and chuckled. He started the truck, drove down the road, past the barns, and out to the two-lane blacktop, then he turned to head for the restaurant.

"You said you hadn't worn heels that high in a long time. Do you wear any while you're at work?" he asked as he kept his eyes on the road.

"I do some days, but there are days I have to do a lot of running around the hospital. Meetings, luncheons, things like that, and I wear flats on those days. I love Fridays because it's casual."

"So the rest of the week, you have to dress up?"

"I do. I usually wear skirts," she said.

"Yep, trying to kill me," he murmured but grinned when she laughed again.

Once they were inside the restaurant and seated at the table, he had trouble keeping his eyes off her. Every time she'd take a bite of food, he'd watch her lips slide off that fork. And he wanted to feel them on him...everywhere.

The stupid bastard she'd been with had been a

fool. But then, any man who beat a woman was no man in his book. They were cowards. Put them up against a real man, and they'd back down. Sawyer remembered how Tess's ex had backed down from Sam. Ryan Kirkland got what he deserved when Sam put a bullet in his head.

Sawyer wasn't sure when Cory would show up, but like Piper thought, he was sure he would. A man like him didn't give up, especially when he felt he owned the woman. Sawyer mentally snorted. No man *owned* a woman. She wasn't a piece of furniture or a pet. His father had always taught him and his brother that women were to be treated with respect. Women were hard to understand, but Sawyer would never disrespect them. Not even Marcia after what she'd done. He was angry with her, but no matter how mad he'd been, he had never raised his hand to her.

"Where are you?"

Startled, Sawyer looked at Piper and grinned.

"Just thinking."

"About work?"

"About you and women in general."

Piper sat back in the chair. "What about us?"

"How you should be treated right." He leaned forward. "I know he's going to come looking for you, and I'm telling you I won't let him hurt you if I can help it."

He watched her blink her eyes quickly.

"Thank you," she whispered.

"No problem, darlin'. If I'm anywhere around and he tries, he's going to regret it."

"I appreciate it. He will come looking. I can promise you that."

"We'll be ready. I'll have my employees look out

83

for him too. I won't tell them why, but if you give me a photo of him, I'll let them know he is not to be on the property. I'll make sure Peta knows too. All right?"

"Yes. I'm sure Sam can get a photo for you," she said with a smile, then they continued eating. "By the way, how did you get reservations so quickly? I would think a place like this would be hard to get into."

"It is, but I know the owner," Sawyer said with a smirk.

"It's nice to have friends in high places, huh?"

"Yep. Do you like country music?" He watched a frown mar her brow. She was probably wondering at the question.

"I do. Why?"

"Because Grant Hunter owns this restaurant." He watched as her mouth dropped open.

"You know Grant Hunter?"

"I do. He was born and raised in Clifton and lives there now."

"He lives in Clifton?"

"Yes, ma'am." Sawyer tilted his head.

"How long have you known him?"

"Years. I'm seven years older than he is, but he hung out in Clifton at the diner a lot before he left when he turned eighteen. Most of us know him fairly well. He's a great guy." Sawyer shrugged. "He never let his status go to his head. Hell, he had buses pick up a bunch of us to see him in concert in Billings. It's just the man he is. In fact, he's throwing a party next Saturday night for his wife's birthday, and I've been invited. I can take a date. Care to go?"

"I would love to."

"Great. He's having it at Dewey's."

Sawyer reached across the table and touched her hand, making her look at him.

"You're not going to throw me over for him, are you?" he asked with a grin.

She laughed. "No. Unless he suddenly becomes available."

"Not funny, darlin', not funny."

When they finished with their dinners, the server asked if they wanted dessert, but they declined. Sawyer stood, removed his wallet to get his credit card, and handed it to the server. When she brought it back, he added a tip and looked at Piper.

Let's get out of here, darlin'."

After dinner, he drove up to her cabin, parked, got out then strolled around the front to her side. He opened the door, put his hand out for her, and smiled when she placed hers in his. She stepped onto the running board and stared at him. Sawyer couldn't stop himself from cupping her face in his hands and leaning in to kiss her. God! She was beautiful, and he wanted her like no other.

She smiled at him, stepped off the running board, and led him inside the cabin. He removed his hat and placed it on the bench by the back door.

"Would you like some coffee?" she asked him.

"I would, thank you." He pulled a chair out from the table and took a seat.

He watched her walk to the K-cup machine, add the cup, press brew, and turn to look at him. He couldn't take his eyes off her, and he grinned when a sexy smile lifted her lips as she walked to him, and he shot to his feet.

"I'll take that bet, Sawyer," she whispered as she placed one hand on his cheek and the other on his chest and gazed up at him.

"Are you sure?"

"Are you backing out of a bet?"

Grinning, he shook his head. "No way. I just want you to be sure this is what you want."

"Oh, I'm sure. I've never been more sure of anything in my life. Unless you think you'll lose."

He laughed. "I'm very confident that *you're* going to lose."

Piper took a deep breath, held her hand out to him, and he took it.

"I know we don't know each other very well, but I trust you, Sawyer. I know you'd never do anything I didn't want you to."

He tugged his hand from hers and cupped her face in his hands.

"I promise you I never will." He lowered his lips to hers.

He deepened the kiss and moved his tongue deep into her mouth, and groaned when she moved hers against it.

After breaking the kiss, she took his hand and led him down the hallway to her bedroom.

They entered the room, and she led him close to the bed then stared up at him. He took in her beautiful face, then stared at her lips. He stepped closer, and their eyes met.

"Are you absolutely sure about this, Piper?"

"Sawyer, I think you're the one who's not sure."

"Hell, darlin', I've been sure since I first saw you."

"Me too. I ran into the back of Trevor because I was looking at you," she said with a laugh.

"Is that so? Well, I admit, I wanted you the minute I saw you. When I asked you if you were married or involved with anyone, I held my breath waiting to hear that answer, and I prayed it was no."

"No man has ever looked at me like you do, Sawyer." She smiled up at him. "I hope I lose that bet."

"Trust me, sweetheart, you will." He picked her up, placed her in the center of the bed, and lay beside her. "You're so beautiful," he whispered before taking her lips in a deep kiss.

****

Piper loved the way he kissed. All in. His lips moved across her cheek to her ear, where he tugged on the lobe with his teeth, making her shiver. He raised his head and stared into her eyes. She placed her hand on his cheek.

"Are you sure?"

Piper blew out a laugh. "I swear, Sawyer Griffin, you are trying to get out of this."

"Oh, hell no. I just don't want you to regret it."

"I won't, I promise. Please."

His head lowered. He placed his lips over hers, moved his tongue into her mouth, and she moved hers against his, making him groan. His hand moved down her side to the bottom of her dress, then he moved it under the material up to the outside of her thigh. She held her breath as his hand moved up to her hip and cupped it in his hand. He skimmed his lips across her cheek to her ear.

"Want to keep those shoes on?" he whispered.

"If you want me to."

"Ever since I saw you wearing them, I wanted them hooked behind my back. I'm so fucking hard. I hope I can make it out of my jeans."

She burst out laughing and ran her hand down from his broad shoulders to his chest, then to the fly of his jeans. He sucked in a breath.

"I sure hope you do because this," she squeezed him through the denim, "feels amazing."

Sawyer pressed his lips to hers and forced them wider apart. His hand moved across the front of her panties, making her hold her breath.

"Relax, baby. I'll never do anything you don't want me to. You can tell me no right now, and I'll leave."

"No way am I telling you no," she whispered.

"Sit up," he demanded.

She sat up, and his hand reached around the back to lower the zipper on her dress, then he lowered it to her waist. Her red demi-cup bra was all lace, and she hoped he liked it. His eyes closed for a few seconds, opened, and stared into hers.

"You are so gorgeous." He ran the tip of his finger along the top of her breast.

Reaching behind her, she took a deep breath, unclasped the bra, then drew the straps down her arms, lowered the bra, and threw it.

"Holy shit, darlin'. You are perfect." He put his hand on her shoulder and slowly pushed her back down. She watched as his eyes roamed over her breasts. Then he leaned down, took a nipple into his mouth, and sucked. When he ran his tongue around the nipple, she thrust her fingers into his thick hair. His thumb moved around the nipple on her other breast, then he switched.

Dear God! Was she going to survive this? Cory never took time like this. It was all about him. Mentally shaking her head, she didn't want to think of him at a time like this. He'd done none of this, and it seemed like the sex was always over before it really got started.

"Touch me," Sawyer whispered against her breast.

She slowly moved her hands over his shoulders to his back. She tugged his shirt out from his jeans, pulled it up, making him raise his head, then she threw it to the floor and ran her fingers through the soft hair on his chest and down to his six-pack stomach, and then his belt buckle. She moved her hand inside the waistband and touched the tip of his hard cock with her thumb. Sawyer groaned.

"I want you so much, Sawyer," she whispered.

"Oh, baby, I want you too." He rolled away from her, sat on the side of the bed, toed off his boots, and pulled off his socks. He grabbed his wallet from the back pocket of his jeans, removed a condom, then shucked his jeans and boxer briefs.

When he turned to face her, his hard cock jutted out, and she couldn't help but moan. She lifted her hips and pushed her dress off but left her panties on. She wanted him to take them off.

She watched as he walked to the bottom of the bed and stared down at her. He didn't take his eyes off her as he ripped open the packet and rolled the condom down over his hard shaft. She had never seen anything sexier. Well, maybe his body, because those abs and that happy trail were making her mouth water. Then he put his knee on the bed, leaned down, kissed her leg, and ran his tongue up her thigh to the elastic of her panties, and kissed her belly.

"Look at me," he said.

She raised her head and stared into his beautiful eyes.

"I'm going to taste every inch of you," he said as he removed her panties, tossed them to the floor, and lowered his face to her curls.

Piper about jumped off the bed when his tongue moved along her slit. She fisted her hands on the sheets. He spread her legs with his shoulders and placed his mouth over her clitoris, and sucked. One of his hands moved up her belly to her breast, where he lightly squeezed while he sucked on her. Oh, God! She'd never felt anything so wonderful in her life. A feeling rushed over her, and she couldn't catch her breath.

"Let go, Piper. I'll catch you."

Piper screamed as she came and threw her hand over her mouth. She had never screamed during sex before. As she was coming down from her high, she felt him moving up her body. He took her lips in a deep kiss, and she could taste her essence on his lips.

"Ready?" he asked when he raised his lips from hers.

"Yes, please," she pleaded and gasped when he inched into her.

He let her adjust to his size and moved in a little more. When he was buried as far as he could go, she wrapped her legs around his waist, making him groan.

When his hips moved, she moved hers in rhythm with him. His hand slipped under her and pulled her tight against him as he picked up the pace. That feeling came roaring over her again. Throwing her head back on the pillow, she bit her lip.

"Let it out, Piper. I want to hear you scream my name," he said against her lips.

It threw her over, and she did as he asked. He

placed his face in the crook of her neck and groaned as he came. He took deep breaths, then lifted his head to look at her.

"You okay?"

"Wonderful," she murmured.

Sawyer laughed. "Yes, you are. So, I win the bet, huh?"

"No."

"*What?*" he said as he reared back.

"If I say you lost, we'd have to keep doing that until you won."

Sawyer burst out laughing. "Oh, sweetheart, trust me. We'd keep doing that no matter who won."

She laughed. "Okay, yeah, you definitely won."

****

The following Friday after work, Piper met with Tess at the shelter. Both Bonner and Stephanie said it was no problem with her getting a dog. Especially since Stephanie had told Bonner about Cory.

"Take a stroll down the aisles and see what catches your eye," Tess told her.

"All right." Piper walked down the row of cages and just wanted to cry. She'd take them all if she could. They all looked at her with such hope on their furry faces that she hated to choose just one.

As she passed by a cage, she glanced in, then stopped, backed up, and looked in at the large dog sitting in the corner. She squatted down and tried to get the dog to come to her, but it wouldn't budge, and it looked so very sad.

"Come on, baby, I won't hurt you," she whispered as she looked at the black and brown dog. She put her fingers through the wire and wiggled them.

"That's Lola. She was abandoned. Her owners left town, and they left her chained in the backyard, though she is house trained. I think they didn't want to leave her in the house when they took off."

Piper could hear the anger in Tess's voice, and she couldn't blame her.

"How do you know she's house trained?"

"Because her owners brought her to me for shots since she was a pup, and I remember Phyliss telling me she'd gotten Lola house trained. I am just so disappointed that they did this to her. She's a wonderful dog, and she has no clue why she's here."

"She's a big girl."

"Yes, she's part Rottweiler and English Mastiff. The thing is, I don't think she's done filling out yet. She's only two, and she'll probably get close to one hundred and fifty pounds. Poor baby. I'd take her, but Sam would have a fit. We have enough right now."

Piper looked back at the dog. "Come here, Lola. You're such a pretty girl."

"She's spayed too."

"I want her, but I need to get her to come to me."

Tess lifted a leash off the hook, moved around her, opened the gate, and moved inside.

"She may look intimidating, but she's a pussycat." Tess rubbed the dog's ears, and Piper watched as Lola closed her eyes in bliss. "Come on, sweetheart, you deserve a good home."

Tess hooked the leash on Lola's collar then led her out of the cage. The dog sat down in front of Piper.

"Hi, big girl," Piper crooned, then giggled when Lola licked her face.

Tess laughed. "I think she knows you're going to take her home."

Piper looked up at Tess with tears in her eyes.

"I don't know how someone could just leave an animal behind."

"It happens way more than it should. I see it all the time. That and abused animals, and I get so pissed, I could take a whip to some people. That is one part of Sam's job he hates. He has seized a lot of abused animals."

Nodding, Piper got to her feet, took the leash from Tess, and led Lola out to the counter to pay for her. She handed over her debit card, told the woman at the counter to add more for a donation. Then after she signed the receipt, she put her card back into her purse. She led Lola to her SUV, opened the back door, and smiled when the dog jumped inside. She turned to hug Tess.

"Thank you."

"Of course. Lola should be enough to scare anyone away. Oh, how did dinner go with Sawyer?"

"I took the bet...and lost," she said, laughing.

"Oh, my. I had a feeling you would. You should call him and ask him to your place for dinner again. Introduce him to Lola." Tess grinned.

"Actually, he is coming to dinner tonight. Thanks again, Tess."

"Sure thing."

"Oh, he invited me to go to a party Saturday night that Grant Hunter is throwing."

"Fantastic. Sam and I will be there too. Hey, we'll talk soon. I'm meeting Sam for dinner at the diner."

Piper smiled as she watched Tess get into her vehicle and drive out of the parking lot. Then she climbed into the driver's seat of her own vehicle and drove home. Lola stuck her head between the front seats and licked the side of her face.

"I'm not going to have to wash my face with you around, Lola." She let out a little squeal when Lola tried to lick her again.

Reaching over, she pulled her phone from her purse and called Sawyer.

"Hey, darlin'," he said when he answered.

"You're still coming to dinner tonight, right? I have someone I want you to meet."

"Someone to meet? Who?"

"Nope, come to the house to meet her."

"Her, huh? Okay, I'll see you at six."

"Sounds good. I'll see you then." She disconnected the call.

Smiling, she laid the phone down and glanced into the rearview mirror to see nothing but Lola's head, making her laugh. She drove up the driveway, slowed by the barns, and looked to see if she saw Stephanie or Bonner. She wanted to introduce them to Lola, but she didn't see them anywhere. Shrugging, she drove up to her small cabin, parked, and opened her door. When Lola barked, Piper grinned.

"No one should come around once they hear that bark. I'll be right back."

She popped the back hatch and lifted out the dog food. She'd get the chew toys and bowls on the second trip. She'd purchased everything before going to the shelter because she knew she would come home with a dog. She just didn't expect it to be the size of a pony.

After putting everything inside, she headed back for the SUV and opened the back door to let Lola out. She had left the leash attached to her collar, so she led her up the steps and into the cabin. She loved this little bungalow. It had been where Bonner lived when he'd been the ranch manager at Caroline's Dream, the ranch's name.

The little cabin contained a kitchen with a bar separating it from the living room. The large stone fireplace took up one wall with a TV hanging above the mantle. A blue sofa faced the hearth, and an overstuffed chair sat in front of the window. The solid wood door led to a covered front porch, and a hallway led to two bedrooms and a bathroom. She loved the home.

Unhooking the leash from Lola's collar, she watched as the dog sniffed around the kitchen then headed for the living room with Piper following her. Lola ran down the small hallway to the bedroom and bathroom. When she came out of the bathroom, she sat down in front of Piper and barked.

"I'm glad it meets your approval. Come on, let's get you some food, then I need to make dinner. I have a very hot man coming here tonight, and to meet you. Please be nice, okay?" She smiled when Lola barked again.

They made their way back to the living room, where Lola plopped down on the floor in front of the fireplace.

"I'll be right back, Lola. I need to get your toys and bowls so I can feed you."

After making a quick trip to her SUV, Piper entered the kitchen and headed to the living room. Lola hadn't moved, but when Piper squeezed the toy, making it squeak, the dog perked her ears, sat up, and wagged her tail. Piper smiled and tossed it to her. Lola caught it and laid back down to chew on it.

Piper turned and headed to the kitchen to start dinner. She hoped Sawyer liked spaghetti because it was quick to make, and she already had hamburger thawed. She chopped an onion, tossed it into a frypan, and filled a big pot with water. As the onions simmered, she added the burger, stirred it, drained the grease, and added the sauce. Setting the lid on the frypan, she turned the burner to simmer and filled the dog dishes with food and water, then headed for the living room to check on Lola and found her asleep on the floor. Piper smiled as she looked at her. She hoped Lola would love her new home.

Piper headed for her bedroom to change out of her jeans. She stripped off her clothes, pulled on her lounge pants and a T-shirt, and then pulled on a pair of socks.

Making her way to the kitchen, she stirred the sauce and made some garlic bread. She'd wait for Sawyer to get here before she added the spaghetti to the water once it started boiling. Looking at the clock, she saw it was later than she thought. He should be here soon. Too bad he couldn't spend the night, but he had to meet with someone tomorrow morning about getting their horse started at the ranch. She put the garlic bread on the cookie sheet and slid it into the oven.

She smiled when she heard a vehicle pull up then jerked when Lola ran into the kitchen barking.

"Good heavens, you're going to be one hell of a watchdog. Now hush," she said and smiled when Lola quit barking and sat. "Good girl."

Walking to the door, she opened it to see the sexiest man she'd ever seen standing there. He grinned, leaned down, kissed her, and lurched back when Lola barked.

"Good Lord! What's a horse doing in the house?" he teased as he took his hat off and placed it on the bench.

"This is who I wanted you to meet. This is Lola. I adopted her today."

"They didn't have any bigger dogs?"

"You're funny, Griffin."

"She definitely has some Rottweiler in her, and I'd say some Mastiff."

"Yep, Rottie and English Mastiff."

Sawyer laughed and shook his head. "She should keep any strangers away."

"But not you." Piper wrapped her arms around his neck and kissed him.

"I sure as hell hope not, darlin'."

"I hope you like spaghetti."

"I love it, and I'm starving. I skipped lunch today, and it smells fantastic. Almost as good as you," he said as he put his face in the crook of her neck.

"Go have a seat, and I'll start the spaghetti. Take Lola with you."

"Yes, ma'am. C'mon, Lola, let's get acquainted."

Piper smiled as she watched them leave the kitchen. It seemed like Lola was going to work out just fine. She seemed to like Sawyer, and she'd always thought if your dog didn't like someone, you shouldn't either. Same with horses. It still amazed her that Frick snapped at Cory anytime he was near the horse but had only snapped at Bonner because he had been in pain.

"How's Frick doing?" she called out.

"Great. He should be good to go in a few days. He loves the treadmill."

Piper nodded even though Sawyer couldn't see her. She should really thank Tess for suggesting taking the horse to Sawyer. Otherwise, she might not have met him. Thank God she did! That man was hotter than hell and did know what to do with a woman, just like he'd told her.

Once the spaghetti was ready, she put some on each plate, then topped it with the meat and sauce just as the oven beeped, signaling the garlic bread was ready.

Putting an oven mitt on her hand, she opened the oven door, pulled the cookie sheet out, and placed it on the counter. She reached for a spatula, put a slice of bread on each plate, and placed the plates on the table.

After taking the mitt off, she tossed it onto the counter and headed for the living room. She came to a stop and laughed when she saw Sawyer on the floor, wrestling with Lola.

"Who's winning?" she asked.

"I don't mean to offend the lady here, but she's too big for me to get the better of."

"Well, you two will have to stop for a while. Dinner's ready."

"Yes, ma'am. Let me wash up, and I'll be right there."

Sawyer got up from the floor and headed down the hallway. Lola stared after him, then looked at Piper.

"Yeah, I know. He's sexy, huh?" Piper laughed as Lola looked back down the hallway. Piper walked back to the kitchen.

"This is a nice little cabin. I didn't ask the last time I was here, but how many bedrooms?" Sawyer asked as he entered the kitchen.

"Two. One I have my treadmill in."

Sawyer sauntered to her and wrapped his arms around her.

"Not the one I'm interested in, sweetheart," he murmured and put his face in the crook of her neck.

"You don't want to use the treadmill?"

He chuckled against her neck. "I have another form of exercise in mind."

"We'll discuss it. Please sit down and eat."

"Yes, ma'am." But he stood beside the table.

"Please have a seat, Sawyer."

"I will, after you."

Piper shouldn't be surprised that he had manners. Most men she'd met in this area did. She sure wasn't used to that. Smiling, she pulled a chair out and took a seat. Sawyer sat down across from her. She looked at Lola to see her sitting beside his chair.

"I think you have a friend. Lola lay down." The dog huffed and dropped on the floor.

"It looks like she listens well. I think you have a wonderful dog there."

"Tess said she was abandoned." Piper watched as Sawyer clenched his jaw.

"I don't get some people. If you don't plan on keeping an animal, don't get one."

"I totally agree."

Sawyer nodded, picked up his fork, and dug into his food. He placed a forkful into his mouth, chewed, swallowed, and looked at her.

"Damn good, darlin'."

"Thank you," she said and knew her cheeks were beet red.

"You're not used to compliments of any kind, are

you?"

"No."

"Well, get used to it. I'd like to kick your ex's ass."

"You might get the chance if he comes here looking for me."

Sawyer set his fork down. "I told you, we'll be ready for him."

"I think he'll do whatever he can to find me," she whispered.

"If it's in my power, I won't let him hurt you. I know I told you that before, but I want you to know that I mean it." Sawyer reached across the table and touched her hand.

"Thank you. It's one reason I wanted a big dog."

"Big is an understatement with this girl." Sawyer grinned.

"Cory hates dogs. Hell, I think he hates all animals, but I also think the feeling is mutual."

"Animals have great instincts. Do you have a gun?"

Piper gasped. "No, and I don't want one."

"You should have one. Open carry is legal in Montana, but you would need a permit for concealed. Better safe than sorry. I'll teach you how to shoot."

"No."

"All right, but if you change your mind, I can show you how to use it."

"I won't change my mind."

"Yes, ma'am." He didn't say more, just picked up his garlic bread and took a bite.

Piper hated guns. They scared her. What if it went off accidentally, and she hurt someone or herself? She'd never be able to live with herself if she hurt someone or even an animal. No, she did not want a gun. That was settled. Nibbling on her bottom lip, she wondered if she *would* feel safer having one. She could keep it on the nightstand beside her bed, and if Cory found her, she'd be ready for him. There was no way she'd let him get close enough to hurt her again. A gun might scare him away, along with Lola. She looked up at Sawyer to see him staring at her.

"They scare me," she whispered.

"Yes, and it will scare him, too. Handled properly, there is nothing to be afraid of. I promise I'll teach you how to use it correctly. I don't like the idea of you being here alone. I know Lola is here, but what if he shows up and waits until you let her out, and then he makes his move? Or when you walk out of the hospital after work. You need protection. If I'm close to you, he won't get near you, and I know Lola won't let him close, but we can't be with you twenty-four seven."

"I know. I'll think about it."

"It's all I can ask."

They continued to eat in silence, and she noticed he cleaned his plate up. He sat back and groaned.

"I ate too much," he said, rubbing his flat stomach.

"I didn't ask you to eat all of it."

"It would be rude not to finish what you put on my plate, so it's your fault."

Piper laughed. "Yeah, you keep telling yourself that."

Sawyer winked at her, pushed his chair back, stood, and carried his plate to the sink. When he came back to the table, he stood beside her chair.

"Are you finished?"

"Yes, but I can—"

"Sit. You cooked. I'll clean up." He reached around her, picked up her plate and fork then carried them to the sink.

Piper shook her head. She could get used to this. That was something she couldn't do. She didn't know if she'd have to run again, and as much as she'd hate to leave this town, and especially this man, she knew it could come to it. Pushing her chair back, she stood and walked to the sink to stand beside him.

"Just hand them to me after you rinse them, and I'll load them in the dishwasher."

He turned to look at her, leaned his hip against the counter, and folded his arms.

"I said I'd do it. Go sit down. I am a man, but I do know how to load a dishwasher."

She grinned up at him, stood on her toes, and quickly kissed his lips.

"Okay. I'll be in the living room...waiting."

"Damn," he muttered, making her laugh as she walked out of the kitchen.

She took a seat on the sofa, picked up the remote, aimed it at the TV, and turned it on. Leaning her head back, she closed her eyes. She must have drifted off because the sound of Lola growling made her jerk awake, and she laughed when she saw Sawyer on the floor with the dog again, trying to get the better of her. He wasn't having much luck. He grunted when Lola laid across him. Piper laughed when Lola put her enormous head on Sawyer's chest and panted hard.

"I think you wore her out."

"I don't think I can move now," Sawyer said from where he was sprawled on the floor.

"I fell asleep. I must be more tired than I

thought," she said around a yawn.

Sawyer shoved Lola off him, got to his feet, and took a seat beside Piper on the sofa.

"I need to get going anyway, darlin'. It's getting late, and I have that appointment tomorrow morning."

"Early?"

"Yes, around seven. Only time he could come by. I'll fit anyone in when needed." He reached out and touched her hair.

"I didn't realize it was so late," she said as she looked at the clock to see it was close to ten.

"You had a nice nap while I kept Lola entertained." Sawyer grinned.

"I'm so sorry."

"Don't be, sweetheart. We'll have other nights, right?"

"You can count on it, cowboy."

"Good. I'm going to wash my hands, then I'll get going." He got to his feet and headed down the hallway to the bathroom. A few minutes later, he reentered the living room. "Walk me to the door," he said as he put his hand out to her.

Piper took his hand, and he tugged her to her feet, cupped her face in his hands, and pressed his lips to hers. When he deepened the kiss, she wrapped her arms around his waist, and his hands went to her butt to pull her tight against him. He raised his head, kissed her forehead, took her hand in his, and walked to the back door. He picked up his hat, put it on his head, and tugged the brim low, and pulled her behind him as he moved to the door.

She felt horrible for falling asleep on him when she'd been hoping they'd end up in her bed. Nibbling on her lip, she tugged on his hand to stop

103

him. He turned to look at her with a raised eyebrow.

"I *am* sorry."

Sawyer grinned. "Don't worry about it. Hell, who knows, I might fall asleep on you the next time. Oh, and Lola has been out. She just came in right before you woke up, but since we were playing, you might want to let her out one more time."

Piper wrapped her arms around his waist, placed her face in the crook of his neck, and inhaled his aftershave. She kissed his neck, his cheek, and then his lips.

"I'll make it up to you," she whispered.

"I'll hold you to that. I'll pick you up around six-thirty tomorrow. The party starts at seven, but I'd like to get there a little early. Sleep well, sweetheart." He kissed her lips quickly, touched the brim of his hat, opened the door, and stepped onto the porch.

Sighing, Piper followed him out, and after he drove off, she let Lola out. Once the dog did her business, Piper opened the door, and they went back inside. She locked the door, turned out the porch light, and headed for the bathroom with Lola on her heels.

She pulled the blankets back, crawled in, and tugged them up to her chin. She let out a squeal when Lola jumped on the bed and plopped down, making the whole bed shake. Piper raised her head to look at her, but she had her eyes closed, and Piper knew there was no way she'd get her to move.

She turned on her side with a smile and thought about the beautiful blouse she had purchased for the party. It was dark chiffon with pink flowers, a square neckline, and short sleeves, and she planned to wear skinny jeans with white stilettos.

She couldn't wait to see what Sawyer thought of her outfit. She closed her eyes and fell asleep.

****

At six-thirty the following evening, Sawyer pulled up to the cabin, parked, and stepped out. He climbed the steps, knocked, and grinned when Lola barked, but the smile left his face when the door opened, and Piper stood there in a beautiful blouse and jeans. His eyes roamed over her, and when they landed on those shoes, he groaned.

"I take it you like my outfit?"

"You look beautiful, but those damn shoes are going to drive me nuts all evening."

Piper laughed. "I'm glad you like them."

"Like is a damn understatement, darlin'. Let's go before I change my mind, and we skip the party."

"Oh, no. Do you think I'd miss a chance to meet Grant Hunter?"

"Not even for some great sex?"

"Hmmm, well, that is a tough decision," she said and grinned.

"Hell, let's go." He took her hand in his.

"Let me get my purse and turn the light on over the sink."

"Yes, ma'am."

Sawyer couldn't take his eyes off her as he watched her from the doorway. Lola sat on the kitchen floor and kept her eyes on her mistress. Yeah, he knew how she felt.

"I'm ready," Piper said as she walked to him.

"You are simply stunning."

He grinned when a blush moved over her cheeks.

"Thank you, and you look very handsome."

"Why, thank you, ma'am." He took her hand again, waited while she locked the door, and then

105

led her to the truck.

At seven o'clock, he watched as Grant and Jessa entered the bar and everyone cheered.

Sawyer glanced over at Piper to see her staring at Grant, with her mouth agape, and he leaned close to her.

"Catching flies?" he asked.

"Shut up. I've never met a celebrity," she whispered back, making him chuckle.

Sawyer saw Calder standing next to Mitzie and smiling down at her. They looked happy, and Sawyer knew how happy Calder was that he'd finally found the right woman.

Glancing at Piper, he saw her talking with Tess, and he wondered if this thing with Piper would amount to anything. He knew her ex would show up, but what about afterward? All he knew was he wanted to find out.

****

Later, Piper glanced around at the crowd. It looked like everyone in the three towns was here. She smiled when she watched Sawyer weave through the crowd, carrying drinks to the table she sat at with Tess, Sam, Bonner, Stephanie, and Holt and Sloane James.

Piper still couldn't believe she was at a party Grant Hunter threw for his wife, and Kay O'Malley was also here.

She smiled when Sawyer took her hand in his.

"Are you having a good time?"

"I am. I can't wait to tell my aunt about this. She's a big fan of Grant's."

"Well, I'm glad to hear you're not," Sawyer said with a grin.

"Oh, no. I can't stand the man," Piper said and

laughed.

"Good thing, because he's heading this way, and I don't want you to go crazy over him like Sloane did the first time she met him." Sawyer looked across the table at Sloane.

"Did you have to bring that up, Sawyer?" Sloane said and laughed when Holt pulled her tight against him.

"I thought for sure she'd leave me for him," Holt said with a chuckle.

"Oh, please. Like he'd ask," Sloane said and gave a little squeal when Holt put his face in the crook of her neck and growled.

"Did you go crazy when you met him, Sloane?" Piper asked.

"I will never live it down, but yes. I couldn't even speak looking at the man." Sloane put her hands over her face as everyone at the table laughed.

When Grant, Jessa, Kay O'Malley, and two other people arrived at the table, the men got to their feet, shook hands with Grant, and hugged Jessa.

Piper leaned close to Tess. "Who is the other man?"

"Calder Moore," Tess whispered.

"Good God, that man is gorgeous."

"I heard that," Sawyer said as he turned to look down at her.

Piper chuckled and shrugged. "Well, I did not mean for you to."

He grinned and turned back to Grant.

"Grant, Jessa, this is Piper Howard. Piper, Grant and Jessa Hunter."

Piper got to her feet and shook their hands. Then Sawyer introduced her to Kay O'Malley, and they shook hands.

107

"Nice to meet you. Happy birthday, Jessa," Piper said.

"Thank you. It's nice to meet you, Piper." Jessa smiled at her.

"This is Mitzie and Calder Moore," Sawyer added.

She shook their hands then watched as Grant winked at Sloane, and everyone laughed again.

"Keep it up, and none of you will be allowed in my bakery again," Sloane said with a mock scowl.

"Damn, we'll behave then," Grant said with a chuckle. "Have a good time, everyone. I'm sure we'll be around again later. We need to get to our table."

Piper watched as Grant took Jessa's hand, led her to a table to the right of the stage, and took their seats. She was having such a good time, but she couldn't keep her eyes off Sawyer. Once they got out of here, she was going to go over every inch of that man.

Chapter Five

Monday morning, Sawyer entered the barn to see the handlers already at work. He never had to worry about his crew. They were always on time and did their jobs without any prodding from him. As he headed for his office, he gave them all a nod.

He entered the office, strode around the desk, and took a seat. He turned on the computer to look at the files to see what horse could leave and smiled when he saw Frick was ready. Reaching for the phone, he called Piper's cellphone.

"Hi," she said.

"Hey, darlin'. I'm calling to let you know that Frick is ready to go home."

"That's wonderful. I miss him so much. Can I ride him?"

"Yes, ma'am. He's doing great. Hey, how about leaving him here until the weekend, and we can go on a ride together?"

"I'd love that. Saturday or Sunday?"

"Both. I want you to spend the weekend. Can you come out Friday after work?"

"Yes. I'll pack a bag and see you Friday night, cowboy."

"Can't wait, but no need to pack a bag."

"I can't ride nude, Sawyer."

He could hear the laughter in her voice.

"The ride I'm talking about, you can."

"Stop. You are so bad."

"Yeah, and you love it."

"I do. I'll see you around seven. Oh, can I bring Lola?"

"Of course. I love the big girl already. I'll see you then, sweetheart." He disconnected the call.

After an hour of going over files, he pushed his chair back, stood, and stretched. His back cracked when he arched back.

"Shit. Bones cracking and gray hair." He shook his head, then made his way out of his office.

He enjoyed watching the horses get their workouts. Striding out of the barn, he made his way to the one with the straight-line pools. He opened the door, entered, and made his way to the first pool to see Trevor on one side, and Brick on the other. Both held ropes to lead the horse through the water.

"Hey, boss," Trevor said.

"Trev. Brick, how's it going, guys?" Sawyer folded his arms and watched them.

"Good. This horse loves the water," Brick said with a grin.

Sawyer nodded, then walked on to the next pool, which was a different matter altogether. This horse was panicking. He reared up and pulled against the leads. Sawyer stepped forward, took the rope from one handler, then slowly pulled the horse toward him while he crooned to it. When the horse settled down, Sawyer rubbed its face and talked to the horse quietly.

"I think we need to use the treadmill for this one. Take him over to the other barn, please."

He watched as the handler led the horse from the barn, then taking a deep breath, he strode out the door to head for the stalls. He needed to check on the other horses.

He let his eyes adjust as he entered the barn, then moved to the first gate to look in at the horse.

Buckshot was a big quarter horse, and he belonged to Calder. The horse had been having problems with his knees, and Calder brought him in.

Sawyer opened the gate, entered the stall, and talked to the horse. But he was having none of it. He moved to the corner and put his ears back, and raked his hoof through the straw on the floor. Sawyer reached his hand out to the horse.

"Come on, boy. I won't hurt you. I just want to check your knees."

The horse didn't move as Sawyer stepped closer, but it snorted, and his ears flattened against his head. Sawyer touched the horse's nose then rubbed his hand up and down its face. He was a gorgeous horse with his red coat, black mane, tail, and black up to his knees on all four legs.

Sawyer wasn't sure if this big guy would let him near him enough to look at his knees. He needed to call Calder before he tried this on his own. He made his way out of the stall, pulled his cellphone from his pocket, found Calder's number, and hit *Send.*

"Hey, Sawyer."

"Calder, I might need you to come by. This horse of yours won't let me near him."

Calder chuckled. "I'll be right there."

"Thanks." Sawyer hit *End* then called Peta to let her know Calder would be arriving and to call Trevor when he got to the office to bring him to the barn. He put the phone in his pocket and placed his arms on the gate to stare at the horse.

A few minutes later, he heard the door to the barn open, and he looked over to see Calder striding down the barn aisle with Trevor walking behind him. Sawyer smiled and stuck his hand out to Calder when he reached him. Calder shook it.

"So Buckshot is giving you problems, huh?"

Sawyer was about to answer when he heard Buckshot neigh, and he stuck his head over the gate to look at Calder. He watched as Calder made his way to the stall and rubbed the horse's nose.

"Hey, boy. Are you being difficult?"

Sawyer shook his head when the horse butted his head against Calder's chest. Calder looked at him with a grin. Horses were loyal to their owners.

"I need to check him over, but he won't let me close to him. I'd rather not tranquilize him."

"I'll hold him while you look," Calder said as he opened the stall then put his hand on the halter the horse wore.

"All right." Sawyer entered after him, and while Calder held the halter and talked to the horse, he squatted down and rubbed his hand around each knee. He could feel heat and swelling.

"How old is Buckshot?"

"Ten, but I don't want him in pain. I ride him more than my other horses."

"I think he'd do better with steroid shots, which means I'm going to have to restrain him or give him a sedative. He's jumpy enough around me, and sticking a needle in those joints isn't safe for him or me."

"Do what you have to do, Sawyer. It's probably best to give him a sedative because I seriously doubt he'll like those needles. Hell, I wouldn't."

Sawyer straightened up. "All right. Let's move him to another stall where he won't eat after he wakes up. That can lead to choking since he'll be groggy."

"I've got him. Lead the way."

Sawyer opened the gate, and Calder, along with

the horse, followed him to another stall. Calder led the horse inside.

"Let me get the sedative. I'll be right back."

Sawyer made his way to the room where he kept the medicines and took a bottle of xylazine and a needle out of the medicine cabinet, then inserted the tip of the needle into the bottle to fill it. After putting the bottle back in the medicine cabinet, he locked it and made his way back to the stall. Calder was still talking to Buckshot. The horse seemed calmer, but Sawyer wasn't taking any chances.

"Okay, I got it. This is just a short-term sedative. It will take a little while to work, then I'll give him the steroid shots. He won't be out long. Maybe thirty minutes."

"Whatever you say. You're the doc."

Sawyer chuckled, moved to the horse, put lidocaine on the spot, waited a few minutes for the medicine to work, so he could give him the sedative. Once he did, the men moved out of the stall to wait for the sedative to take effect.

"How have you been?" Sawyer asked. "I didn't get to talk to you at the party."

"Great," Calder said with a grin.

"I'm happy you found someone. Mitzie is a wonderful woman."

"Yes, she is." Calder glanced at him and back to the horse. "I never thought I'd love someone so much. I waited a long time for her."

Calder placed his arms on top of the gate and stared in at his horse.

"I'm glad. With all the women you dated, I wondered if you were ever going to find the right one."

"All the women? Come on, Sawyer, you make it

sound like I had a harem of them."

Sawyer chuckled. "Well, I wouldn't say that, but you did date a lot, Calder."

"Because I was trying to find that special one."

"That's Mitzie."

"I was about to just say fuck it, and when I got too old, just sell the ranch and move into an old folks' home."

Sawyer laughed. "You love that ranch. Hell, you have one of the best cattle ranches around. It would be tough to have to choose between you and Preston."

"I know, but it entered my thoughts because what good did it do me if I didn't have anyone to hand the ranch down to."

"I'm glad you finally found her," Sawyer said.

"Me too. She might drive me crazy some days, but I love her and that damn potty mouth of hers."

Sawyer laughed. "She and Liv must have been separated at birth."

Calder chuckled and nodded. "I wouldn't doubt it."

"Trick's wedding is soon. I'm glad he found someone too," Sawyer said.

"I'm sure everyone is. We all know how much he loved Kaylee. Damn, what a shame that was, but Rayna is damn good for him."

"Yes, she is. I'm sure Kaylee would want him to move on."

"He said she told him that in a dream," Calder said.

"I believe that." Both men were silent for a few seconds.

"Piper seems like a pleasant woman." Calder stared in at the horse.

"She is. I like her."

"Good. You need someone good in your life. Marcia wasn't it."

"No, she wasn't."

"How's Brooke?"

"Great. She's coming home next week. I can't wait to see her."

Calder nodded, and both men watched as Buckshot lowered himself to the sawdust, laid his head down, and was out. Sawyer opened the gate, and both men entered. He used antiseptic soap to clean the area, then picked up the steroid needle, found the joint area, and quickly inserted the needle. Once he finished one knee, he did the other. The men left the stall and waited for Buckshot to wake up. Sawyer never liked leaving a sedated animal alone. He was never sure how a horse would react to waking up and not getting to its feet right away. Either he would watch the horse, or one of his employees would.

"If you're good, I'll get going. I have a hauler coming in an hour," Calder said as he looked at his watch.

"It'll be fine. I'll call you to let you know how he's doing. I appreciate you coming over, Calder. Trevor will take you back to your truck." Sawyer stuck his hand out, and Calder shook it.

"No problem. Hey, let's all get together for dinner one night."

"Sounds good. I'll get with Piper about it."

Calder saluted and strode out of the barn with Trevor while Sawyer monitored Buckshot. About thirty minutes later, the horse tried to get to his feet but was still woozy. Sawyer continued to watch him, but he finally stood. He was still out of it a little, but he drank some water and seemed to be coming around just fine.

Sawyer left the barn and headed for his office in the other barn to add this to Buckshot's file. As he made his way to his office, his cellphone rang, and he pulled it from his pocket. He grinned when he saw his daughter's beautiful face.

"Hey, kiddo," he said.

"Hi, Dad. Are you busy?"

"Never too busy for you. How's your studying going?"

Her sigh came across the line, and Sawyer grinned.

"You never told me this was so hard."

"Oh, come on, Brooke. You're a very intelligent woman. You got this."

"I should have gone to med school."

"Then do it. You do what you want."

"Dad, I'm not serious. I want to be a vet, like you, granddad, and Uncle Colson. I love animals."

"I know you do. Are you still coming to visit in two weeks?"

He knew how tough it was to become a vet. Many people don't realize that you had to learn how to do dentistry, surgery, internal medicine, and x-rays plus have experience with animals before even being admitted to vet school because it shows the admissions committee that you have explored the field and are comfortable with certain species, and possess a certain level of animal handling skills. It's difficult, and the pay is not near to what a medical doctor makes, but the feeling of helping animals is well worth it.

"Yes. I can't wait to see you. I miss you, Dad."

"I miss you too."

116

"I just wanted to say hi. I'll see you soon. I love you, Daddy."

"Love you too, Brooke," he said as he entered his office and took a seat behind the desk.

He placed the phone on the desk and thought about introducing his daughter to Piper. He wanted the two special women in his life to know each other. Although he and Piper hadn't been together long, she meant a lot to him already. The sex was fantastic. It had never been better, and he'd thought it was good with Marcia, but with Piper, he wanted her every minute of the day. He wasn't sure if she wanted the same thing, but he hoped so.

Turning his attention to the computer, he entered the information about Buckshot. That was one stubborn animal, but once he saw his master, he was a pussycat.

Sawyer grinned when he thought of Lola. That dog didn't have to do anything but stand there. She was intimidating as hell, but she loved Piper already. Lola knew Piper had saved her and would give her a wonderful home. Animals had a great instinct. Animals were loyal and treated right they would protect you with their lives.

Later, he headed home after a full day and just wanted to relax for the evening. He hated not seeing Piper tonight, but it was hard for them to get together during the week with both of them working. Some evenings, he worked late, and she did too. He'd see her every night if he could. It had been three years since his divorce, and he was ready to fall in love again. Was it with Piper? It could very well be. He liked her a lot already.

Sawyer had been happy in his marriage, and he thought Marcia was too. Still, once she had sex with another man and blamed it on him for not spending time with her, he knew she hadn't been happy since they moved to Clifton, but that was no excuse.

Blowing out a breath, he drove his truck to the garage attached to the house. It kept the vehicle cool in the summer and warm in the winter. He pushed the remote above the visor and waited as the door slid up. He drove inside and pushed the button again to lower it. Once he pulled in and parked, he stepped out, walked up the steps, then entered his kitchen to see Rio sitting there waiting for him.

Sawyer hung his hat up, squatted down, and rubbed the dog's ears. Rio put his paw on his thigh.

"Hey, buddy. Have you been in all day?" Sawyer straightened to get the dog food and fresh water.

After taking care of Rio, he hooked his booted foot around the leg of a chair at the table, pulled it out, and took a seat. Damn, he was tired.

He looked at the clock to see it was close to six. A long day for sure. He just wanted to grab a quick shower, something to eat, watch a little TV, and hit the sheets. He hated hitting them alone, but the weekend would be here soon enough, and he couldn't wait to spend it with Piper.

That was another thing. He never brought women to his home. If sex was involved, it was always at her place. He always figured they'd get ideas if he brought a woman home, and he didn't want that happening. He had no desire for any woman to get ideas about a future for them until Piper. He really enjoyed her company in and out of bed.

With a yawn, he tugged his T-shirt off, toed off his boots, removed his socks, and stood to

118

unbuckle his belt. He unsnapped his jeans and lowered the zipper. He shucked them along with his boxer briefs and carried the clothes into the laundry room, where he tossed them into the hamper. Then he walked naked to his bedroom and into the bathroom. He glanced at the jacuzzi tub and decided to use it rather than taking a shower. The jets would feel good on his tired muscles.

After his bath, he shaved, pulled on a pair of sweatpants and a T-shirt then headed for the kitchen to fix something to eat. He yanked on the fridge door and stood there, staring at the shelves. Nothing appealed to him, but he knew that he'd be hungry later if he didn't eat. A sandwich would have to do. He gathered what he needed, made his sandwich, got himself a glass of ice water, and headed for the living room. He took a seat in the recliner, raised the footrest, turned the TV on, and ate his sandwich.

He glanced at the clock to see it was almost nine, and he was having trouble keeping his eyes open. Damn. Nine o'clock, and he was ready for bed. What the hell?

After eating, he checked the door to make sure he had locked it, slid the panel down over the pet door, and headed for the bedroom. He could watch TV in there for a while.

Making his way to the bedroom, he couldn't stop yawning. Hell, he'll probably fall asleep while watching TV. He pulled the covers back, pushed his sweatpants down, pulled his T-shirt off, and crawled between the sheets. Rio jumped up onto the bed, made a circle, then flopped down, making the bed shake. Sawyer shook his head and laughed when the dog sighed.

Picking up the remote, he aimed it at the TV and watched the news. He jerked awake and swore. He was more tired than he thought.

Turning off the TV, he turned out the light, rolled to his side, closed his eyes, and fell asleep. He knew it would be morning in no time.

****

Piper jerked awake in a cold sweat. She turned on the light and glanced around the room. Lola came running into the room and jumped on the bed. Piper grunted when the dog laid across her lap.

"You do realize you're the size of a pony, right?" She laughed when Lola licked her face. Glancing at the clock on the nightstand, she saw it was three in the morning.

She wasn't sure why she had that dream. Probably all the talk of Cory lately. The thought he could be out there looking for her scared her to death. He'd kill her this time. Of that, she was sure. No one walked away from him. At least, he'd told her *she* never would.

Shoving at Lola until she moved, Piper tossed the blanket off, got out of bed, and made her way to the kitchen. She leaned back against the counter and wondered what she'd do when he showed up. Piper hadn't been surprised to find out he had abused another woman, and no doubt there were more. But they'd probably been too terrified to press charges. One woman had but then refused to testify against him, and he walked out of the courtroom a free man.

Yanking the fridge door open, she reached inside to get a bottle of water. After twisting the cap off, she took a long drink and headed back to the bedroom.

When she entered the room, she came to a complete stop when she saw Lola sprawled across the entire bed. With a smile, Piper moved to the side of the bed, set the water bottle on the nightstand, crawled in the bed, and tugged on the blanket that Lola was lying on. It was like trying to move a truck. She put her feet against the dog and pushed. Lola sighed.

"Lola, I need room in *my* bed, ya know," Piper said with a laugh.

Lola stood, moved a few inches, plopped back down, making the bed shake. Piper pulled the blanket up, rolled to her side, closed her eyes, and prayed for uninterrupted sleep.

The buzz of the alarm awoke her later that morning, and she reached and slapped it to shut it off. With a yawn, Piper sat up, stretched her arms above her head, threw the covers off, got up, and glanced around but didn't see Lola.

"Lola?"

The dog came running into the bedroom and jumped up onto the bed, making it skid on the hardwood floor. Piper laughed and tried to push the dog out of her face, stepped back, and Lola almost fell off the bed. She licked Piper's face as she stood on the bed at Piper's side.

"Come on, I know you have to go out," Piper said.

Lola jumped off the bed and ran out of the room, with Piper following her to the kitchen. She opened the back door, and Lola ran out. Piper stepped onto the porch to watch her. The dog ran around the yard, did her business, and ran back to the porch. She sat beside Piper, looked up at her, and barked. Piper squatted down and rubbed Lola's ears.

"You're such a good girl, aren't you?" She

121

laughed when Lola tried to get closer and knocked her to her butt. "Good Lord, dog. You do not know how big you are, but you are such a sweet girl. Come on, let's go inside. I have to get ready for work."

She got to her feet, opened the door, and entered the house with Lola behind her. Making her way back to her bedroom, she entered the bathroom to wash her face, put makeup on, and get ready for the day. She hated leaving Lola home alone, but it had to be done.

Piper pulled on thigh-high nylons, a red blouse, and a black pencil skirt, then slipped her feet into her red heels. They were only three inches because if she wore any higher, she'd be kicking them off under her desk. She walked back to the kitchen, fixed a cup of coffee, poured it into her insulated travel mug, and walked out onto the porch.

After she locked the door, she headed for her SUV. She aimed the fob at it, climbed in, and drove down the road, past the barns, and out to the road to head for the hospital. She'd call Stephanie later to see if she'd check on Lola for her.

"Please be a good girl, Lola," Piper whispered.

By Friday, she was more than ready to spend some time with Sawyer. She hadn't seen him since last Saturday for the birthday party. He'd ended up working on Sunday and had a long day. She missed him, but she was eager to get home, pack, get Lola, and head to his house. She was so eager to see his home.

After she parked by the porch of her cabin, stepped from her vehicle, she started to climb the steps to head for the door, but she stopped when she didn't hear Lola barking. The dog always

122

barked when she arrived home. Fear overtook her, and she was too afraid to open the door. She backed away from the steps to head back to her vehicle when her cellphone buzzed, making her jerk in surprise. She pulled it from the pocket in her jeans to see Bonner's number.

"Bonner?"

"Hey, I was hoping to get back before you got home. I have Lola with me. When Stephanie checked on her today, she said Lola looked lonely, so she brought her to the barns. I took her with me when I rode up to check the fence. I'm heading back now, then I'll get her in the truck and be right up," Bonner said.

Piper blew out a relieved breath. "Oh, that's fine. I was wondering why she didn't bark when I walked up the steps to the porch."

There was no way she would tell him it had terrified her that Cory had found her and done something to the dog. Although Bonner and Stephanie knew about Cory, she didn't want them feeling bad about scaring her.

"Yeah, that's some watchdog you have. She lets anyone know she's in the house. I'll be at the barn in a few minutes," Bonner said and disconnected.

Piper leaned against her SUV, placed her hand over her chest, and tried to calm her heart. It was beating so hard she was sure it would pop out of her chest. She pushed away from the vehicle, walked to the steps of the porch, and took a seat on the top step. She needed to take a few deep breaths to calm down.

Tears rolled down her cheeks, and she angrily brushed them away. She swore she'd never cry because of that man ever again. She had been so scared when she didn't hear Lola. Cory wouldn't hesitate to hurt an animal if it meant he could get to her.

She wasn't sure how long she sat there when she heard a vehicle coming up the road, so she got to her feet and brushed the back of her jeans off. Shading her eyes with her hand, she looked to see Bonner's truck coming closer.

Sucking in a deep breath, she smiled as she watched him stop the truck by the steps, and Lola started barking. Bonner opened the door, stepped out, opened the back door, and Piper saw Lola jump down from the seat and run to her. She squatted down and hugged the dog. Placing her face against her neck, she blinked back tears.

"Are you all right?"

Piper looked up at Bonner and nodded.

"Yes."

"If you say so." He frowned at her. "Hey, I'm sorry, but I need to get going. We're going out to dinner, and I need a shower."

"Okay. I won't be here all weekend," she said, and the heat poured into her cheeks.

"All right. Are you taking Lola with you?"

"I am. I'll be home Sunday evening." Piper straightened up. "I'm sure Lola had a great time with you today."

Bonner grinned. "She did. She loved running with the horse and Bodie. She had a silly grin on her face the whole time. You need to take her out with you when you ride."

"I will." Piper smiled. "Please tell Stephanie I appreciate her checking on Lola this week. I hated leaving her alone her first week here."

"Hey, we love her. We'll watch her anytime you

want us to. Now Stephanie wants another dog." He shook his head. "I'd better go. Have a good weekend." He turned around to head for his truck. After he climbed in, he put the window down, grinned at her, and touched the brim of his hat. "Tell Sawyer hey for me."

Piper gasped, then grinned when she heard Bonner chuckle. He drove down the driveway and disappeared. She looked down at Lola.

"Did you have a good day? Of course, you did if you spent it with that good-looking man, huh? Not to mention how handsome his dog, Bodie, is." Piper turned from the dog, unlocked the door, and entered the cabin with Lola behind her.

****

Sawyer strode from the barn, glanced at his watch, and swore under his breath. Piper was due any minute, and he needed to grab a shower. He had worked with a tough horse today, and by the time he finally got the horse into the pool, sweat poured off him. He almost jumped into the pool with the horse just to cool off.

As he opened the door on his truck, his cellphone buzzed, and he took it from his shirt pocket to answer. He grinned when he saw Piper's face.

"Hey, you," he said when he answered.

"I'm at the gate. It's locked."

"Damn. I forgot to tell Peta to leave it open. I'll be right there. I'm at the barn, so I'm close."

"All right."

Sawyer hit *End,* climbed into his truck, and drove up to the gate to see Piper standing outside her vehicle. He stepped out of the truck with the key to the lock but stopped when he heard Lola barking from inside Piper's SUV.

"She is definitely a good watchdog," he said as he continued to the gate. He inserted the key, twisted it, opened the lock, and swung the gate open.

"Yes, she is." Piper's head tilted. "Were you going to leave this unlocked for long?"

"No, I was going to come down and lock it after you got here. Figured I'd make sure you couldn't leave before Sunday." He chuckled when her cheeks turned pink.

"You don't have to lock me in to get me to stay," she said.

"Good to know, darlin'. Okay, drive through, and I'll lock it. Then you can follow me to the house. I need to get a shower once we get there."

"Were you working late?"

"Yes, we had a horse that wouldn't cooperate. A female. What a shock," he said with a smile.

"We females can be a little stubborn."

"A little? Big understatement, Piper. *Big* understatement."

She laughed, climbed into her vehicle, drove through the gate, and waited while he locked it. Then he got into his truck and headed for the house with her behind him. He couldn't wait to have her in his home for the weekend. He loved spending time with her. Maybe he'd even let her out of bed once in a while. Long enough to go skinny dipping in his pool at the back of the house. No one would see them. He'd just have to convince her.

He grinned as he thought of doing that. First, he had to get her naked. Shit. He shifted around in the seat as he thought of her being nude. She had one hell of a body, and he loved going over it, which he definitely planned to do as much as possible this weekend.

Once he pulled up to the house, he parked and stepped out. He watched as Piper climbed out of her vehicle, opened the back door, and prepared himself when Lola spotted him and ran at him at full speed, but she skidded to a halt and sat down when she reached him. He blew out a relieved breath. She was a great dog, but she thought she was a lapdog. He leaned over and rubbed her ears.

"Hey, pretty girl."

"You looked terrified when she was running at you," Piper said with a laugh.

"She's the size of a small horse, and as much as I love them, I don't want them running at me either." He tilted his head. "What do you have there?" He nodded at the suitcase in her hand.

"I will wear clothes, Sawyer Griffin. You will not keep me naked the entire time I'm here," she said, and a slow smile lifted her lips. "Unless you are too."

He grinned. "Deal. Come on, let's get in out of this heat, and I'll show you my home."

"I love it already. The surrounding trees are beautiful." She glanced around.

Sawyer looked around. The large white farmhouse sat amidst tall maple trees. The only clearing in front was a small yard and driveway in the front. There were no trees in the backyard because of the pool. A wide wraparound porch encircled the entire house, and rows of rocking chairs sat on it. Black shutters surrounded each window, and several chimneys protruded from the roof.

"How many bedrooms?"

"Six. Seven and a half baths, living room, den, office, and a finished basement. Eight fireplaces. The house along with the barns sit on five hundred acres."

"It's gorgeous." She glanced around. "Where is the barn you have for your horses?"

"Right through there." He pointed toward the woods to the right of the house.

"Oh, I see the road now. It's just dirt, so I didn't notice it."

"I either walk to them or drive my truck, so I didn't feel the need to blacktop it. We'll go riding in the morning."

"Sounds good."

"Come on," he said as he strode to her, took the suitcase, leaned down, and quickly kissed her lips. He raised an eyebrow when she leaned back and wrinkled her nose.

"You do need a shower," she said and put her hand over her nose.

Sawyer chuckled. "I told you."

"I'm kidding. You always smell terrific." She put her arms around his neck and pressed her lips to his. He dropped the suitcase and pulled her tight against him.

He slowly raised his lips from hers. "I could skip the shower…"

"Or…I could take one with you."

"Now that sounds like a good idea. I'm anxious to see how Lola and Rio react to each other." He took her hand in his and led her up the steps with Lola following.

"Rio?"

"My dog." He frowned.

"You never mentioned a dog," she said.

128

"I guess it just slipped my mind. He's harmless."
Sawyer opened the door and jerked his chin for her
to go inside. Lola ran in behind her.

****

Once inside the kitchen, Piper glanced around.
It was so pretty with its white cabinets. White
appliances sat nestled between butcher block
countertops. To the right of the door sat a white
storage bench with hooks. She watched as Sawyer
set her suitcase down, removed his hat, hung it on
a peg, then took a seat on the bench, toed off his
boots, and slid them into one of the storage cubbies
under it. He got to his feet, reached behind him,
and tugged off his T-shirt. She bit her lip to keep
from groaning, looking at that chest and six-pack
stomach. Her eyes traveled lower to his belt buckle
and then the fly of his jeans. When he cleared his
throat, she looked up into his eyes and smiled.

"My eyes are up here," he said with a grin.

"Oh, I know. I know where everything is," she
said and laughed when he chuckled.

"Let's get a shower." He picked up the suitcase,
strode to her, took her hand, and led her through a
dining room.

Piper tugged on his hand to stop him, and he
turned to look at her with his eyebrow raised.

"I'd like to see the house," she said and watched
as Lola ran out of the room. "Lola." Piper glanced
around. "Where's your dog?"

"Probably out. He has a pet door he uses. It's in
the laundry room off the kitchen. Lola's fine. She
can't hurt anything." He huffed. "All right. Dining
room," he said as he pointed to the cherry table in
the center of the room.

A large hutch with mirrors behind the glass

shelves sat against one wall, and a buffet sat under a row of windows. The dark walnut hardwood floor was the same as the kitchen. He tugged on her hand and led her into the living room. She couldn't seem to catch her breath as she glanced around.

A large brick fireplace with rows of bookshelves on each side took up the entire outside wall. A soft beige covered the walls. Above the mantle hung a deer's head. She pulled her hand from his, walked to the fireplace and stared up at the deer then turned to look at him.

"Did you shoot him?"

"Uh, yeah," he muttered.

"A fourteen-point," she said. "He's gorgeous."

"You worried me there for a minute. I thought you were going to be angry about it. You know how some people say I'm killing Bambi."

"They don't understand that it's the most humane for the deer. I know because my uncle hunts. When I was a little girl, I was so mad at him for shooting one, but then he explained that they are so overpopulated that it's this way or they die of starvation." She turned to look at him. "You eat the meat, though, right?"

"Of course. I don't hunt for trophies."

"Good."

"I've gone on elk hunts with Noah Conway in Kalispell, but I've never been fortunate enough to get one."

"Who is Noah?"

"He's a good friend and one of the best saddlers you'd ever meet, but he also has land in Kalispell that he takes hunting groups on. He's a guide. It's fun but always cold as hell. I've gone several times. His one rule is no trophy hunting. He makes everyone sign a waiver. If they don't want the meat, it's donated to homeless shelters."

"Wasn't he at the party?"

"No. He probably had some deadlines to meet."

"Well, maybe the next time you go to Kalispell, you'll get one."

"I hope so." He glanced over his shoulder toward the kitchen. "I think Rio just came in."

A large dog came running into the room and skidded to a halt when he saw Lola. Piper watched as Lola stared at him, then she started wagging her tail, and Rio did the same. Then they ran around the living room.

"I guess he's not even interested in me," she said with a laugh.

"That's okay, darlin', I am."

Piper grinned at him, then turned to look at the room again. She could see the front porch from the row of windows that had a window seat under them. A large flat-screen TV sat in the corner next to the windows. A recliner and overstuffed chair faced it, and a sofa with a coffee table in front of it faced the fireplace. To her right was the foyer. The white entry door had four large panes of glass to let the light shine in, and a grandfather clock sat catty-corner next to it. She headed that way to see a set of stairs leading to the second floor, with a landing halfway up. Across the foyer was a hallway that she walked to and saw two other doors.

"The office and den are down that hallway, along with a bathroom. There's a half-bath under the stairs, and the hallway beside them leads back to the kitchen. There is also a swimming pool out back."

"A swimming pool?"

"Yes, ma'am. Maybe we'll take a swim tomorrow after our ride." He grinned.

"I'd love it, though I didn't bring anything to swim in."

Sawyer laughed. "I know."

Piper swatted at him. "You are so bad. Where are the other fireplaces?" she asked as she watched Lola sniffing around the foyer.

"Each bedroom has one, this one here." He pointed to the one in the living room. "And the den has one."

"You have a beautiful home, Sawyer."

He sauntered to her. "Thank you. Let me show you the upstairs."

He took her hand, led her to the stairs, and climbed them with Lola and Rio following them. At the top, Piper looked down a long hallway and saw three doors on one side and four on the other.

"Three bedrooms on each side, with the full bath on this side." He pointed to the left.

"It's an enormous house. How old is it?"

"My dad's great-great-grandfather built it in the eighteen hundreds when he was in his early twenties. Since Brooke is my only child, I will pass it to her."

"It's had to have gone through a lot of renovations over the years."

"Oh, yeah. I did a lot of them after I moved in. Come on, let's shower." He grinned.

She followed him to a room. He opened the door and jerked his chin for her to enter, and she gasped when she did. The largest bed she'd ever seen sat against the far wall. A matching chest of drawers sat beside sliding glass doors that led to a balcony, and a dresser sat on the opposite wall with a row of bi-fold doors beside it. The fireplace faced the bed with a door alongside it. Since it was open, she walked to it and peered in. The bathroom looked bigger than the cabin she lived in. The shower stall took up the entire back wall with stone on three sides, and the front was glass. The white tub was huge and also surrounded by stone, and a window sat above it. Piper looked back at him.

"I love it."

"Thanks. One of the renovations I made. Some days I need that jacuzzi to make these old muscles feel better." He grinned.

"You're not old." She walked to him and wrapped her arms around his waist, and stared up into his handsome face. "I'd rather get in the jacuzzi."

"Later. I need that shower, then we'll get something to eat."

"Can we go to the Hartland Restaurant?" she asked as she stepped back from him.

A frown marred his brow. "If you want..."

Piper shrugged. "I just thought Grant would be there," she said and squealed when Sawyer pulled her to him and pressed his lips to hers.

"I need to take your mind off Grant," he said when he raised his lips.

"Grant who?" She laughed when he grinned at her. "Let's get that shower, then we'll talk about dinner."

"Yes, ma'am." Sawyer kicked the door shut.

Chapter Six

When they were in the barn saddling the horses, Saturday morning, Sawyer was anxious to show her his land. There were riding trails all over the property, then they would enter a field with a big pond.

"I'm taking fishing poles with us. We can stop at the pond and fish a little."

"All right," she said. "You have the lunch I made too, right?"

He nodded as she put the tack on Frick and chuckled when the horse took her hat from her head.

"He did that to me. I was afraid of the condition it would be in when I got it back."

"I hope he didn't damage it," she said as she took the hat from the horse, rubbed his neck, then looked at Sawyer.

"No, I got it back fairly easily. He didn't hang on to it. I think he just took it for the hell of it. A lot of horses will try to take a hat. I had a horse take one of my hats once, toss it down and step on it."

Piper's mouth dropped open. "Seriously?"

"Yep. He did a job on it. I had to buy a new one."

"You should have made his owner buy it."

Sawyer chuckled. "I can't do that. I take risks every day with horses that are brought in. It happens. Anything can happen. They have kicked me, stomped on me, and bit me. Perks of the job," he said as he made sure he attached the big canvas saddlebags to his saddle.

"I'm not sure I'd call them perks."

"Anyone who works with animals knows the risks. I think a dog or two has bitten Tess. I'm sure she's had horses do the same to her."

"Well, let me say I'm glad I'm not a vet."

"Or a farrier. One of my horses tugs on my farrier's shirt every time he's working on him." Sawyer grinned. "Are you about ready?"

"Yes, Frick is all set. This is a beautiful saddle," she said as she ran her hand over the leather.

"Conway saddle. I told you he was good."

"Does he have a factory?"

"No, he makes each one by hand in a barn on his property. It takes him about three months to complete one, and he has a long waiting list. Look at the back of the cantle." He watched her walk around to the back, looked at the cantle, then at him. The metal plate on the cantle had his name on it.

"That's gorgeous." She walked to the stirrup fender and ran her hand over the stitching. "He does all of this by hand?"

"All of it. None better. Brooke has one with her name on it too. I got it for her for Christmas one year."

"I bet she loved that."

"Yeah, she did. She always said she loved mine, so I had Noah make her one. It has blue stitching where all of mine have brown."

"All? How many?"

"I have three that I use. Let's get going, darlin'," he said with a grin. "The fish are waiting."

"All right." She put her foot in the stirrup, grabbed the saddle horn and cantle, then pulled herself up into the saddle.

"Well, that was fun to watch," he said as he

135

vaulted into the saddle without even using the stirrup.

"I know I keep saying it, but you are so bad Sawyer Griffin," she said with a mock glare.

"I am, aren't I?" He chuckled. "Let's head out, darlin'."

"Right behind you."

He nudged his horse, Tabasco, and they headed out of the barn. Sawyer glanced over his shoulder to see Piper following him on Frick, and the dogs ran after them. He was glad to see that Rio and Lola were getting along.

"Your horse is beautiful," she said.

"Spoiled rotten too." The big chestnut horse was a gentle giant and loved his master. The feeling was mutual.

"Is he an American Quarter horse?"

"Yes, ma'am. Seven years old. I've had him since he was born."

"So he was born here?"

"Yep. The dam is black with a white blaze down her face, and the sire is chestnut."

"Do they belong to you too?"

"Yes. We'll probably see them in the pasture when we get there."

"I've never fished," she said out of the blue.

He reined his horse to a stop. The leather creaked as he turned in the saddle to look at her.

"We don't have to fish if you don't want to. I just thought we could relax by the pond."

"I'd like to try it, but I'm not touching a worm." She shuddered.

Sawyer turned back around so she wouldn't see his grin. He nodded.

"Noted." He nudged Tabasco to go.

"You'd better not be laughing, Sawyer."

"No, ma'am."

"Liar," she said, making him laugh.

As they rode along, Sawyer glanced around to see if he noticed any of the fence down. He knew one of his ranch hands had checked it this morning, but it never hurt to check it when anyone was out. He saw nothing amiss. So they rode on.

They crested a knoll, and he reined to a stop. Piper reined in alongside him.

"It's beautiful," she said.

"Yes. Montana doesn't lack in beauty."

"It's a beautiful state. I'm so happy I moved here."

He looked over at her. "Me too, Piper. I couldn't be happier that you did."

She stared at him, and a slow smile lifted her lips.

"Maybe I was meant to be here," she said.

"I believe that. Come on, let's get down there to the pond and relax a little."

They nudged their horses and ran them down to the pond. Once they dismounted, they removed the saddles, blankets, and tack to let the horses graze. Sawyer pointed to the middle of the pasture.

"There are Tabasco's parents."

Piper turned to look at the horses then back to him.

"I can see why he's so gorgeous. Those are two beautiful horses."

"Thanks. I've had them since they were both five years old. I love horses, and I know one man doesn't need as many as I have, but I can't help it."

"How many?"

"Fifteen," he murmured.

She burst out laughing. "You're right. You do have a lot for just one man."

"Well, one belongs to Brooke," he said sheepishly.

"One? Oh, yeah, okay. That makes a difference."

He reached out, pulled her close to him, pressed his lips to hers then slowly raised them.

"You are such a smartass," he said against her lips.

"I am, aren't I?" She threw his words back at him.

Sawyer chuckled. "Let's eat, then we'll fish."

"Okay." She laughed against his lips.

After they walked to the pond, Sawyer removed a blanket from the saddlebag, spread it out on the grass, removed the food, and set it on the blanket. He smiled and nodded his head for her to take a seat on the blanket. She did and grinned up at him, and he wanted to have sex with her right there. Clearing his throat, he sat beside her, and they ate their sandwiches. She had also packed some apples. He watched her take a bite, and she held it out to him to bite it. He grinned.

"Are you tempting me with that apple?"

"Is it working?"

"Yes, but you sure as hell don't need an apple for that. Just a look will do."

Piper chuckled. "Good to know."

Later, Sawyer put a worm on her hook and tried not to laugh at her wrinkling up her nose. He had her sit on the bank, then he handed her the pole. She held it out as if afraid the worm would crawl along it and get on her. He washed his hands off in the water.

"Okay, let me teach you how to fish," he said and

glanced around to see where the dogs were. He grinned when he saw them chasing each other in the field. He turned back to look at Piper.

"All right," she said in a low tone of voice.

"Piper, you don't have to do this. You can just watch me."

"No, I'd really like to try it. I hear people say how relaxing it is."

"It's very relaxing, but you have to be patient." He chuckled. "Brooke isn't at all. She'll cast out, and in less than a minute, she's reeling it back in to cast out again."

Piper grinned. "That sounds like something I would do."

"By the way, I want you to meet her. She's coming here next week."

"I'd like that," Piper said.

"Good." He moved to sit behind her, cradling her between his thighs, wrapped his arms around her, and placed his hands over hers on the pole. "Let out a little line first, like this." He showed her how to let the line out. "Okay, hold the line with your finger, like a trigger. Flip the bail over. That releases the line. Now, pull the rod back, throw it out and let go of the line."

She did as he said, but her line only went to the edge of the bank.

"Oops," she said with a laugh.

"No problem. Let's try again. Reel the line back in, but not all the way to the pole. The other way," he said when she tried to turn the handle the wrong way.

"It feels like it's backward."

"I know, but it's not."

He watched her do it again. This time, the line

hit the water, and she looked over her shoulder at him with a big grin on her face. Hell, he'd do anything to get that smile aimed at him.

"Put a little more into it next time."

The smile left her face, and her eyes narrowed.

"I'm trying," she growled out.

"I know you are, but most of the bigger fish are more toward the center of the pond, not at the bank."

"Whatever," she muttered, making him chuckle.

"Come on, once more." He watched her take a breath, reel in the line, raise the pole, and cast out again. "Better. If you're okay, I'll get my line in the water."

"How will I know when I get a fish?"

"You'll feel a tug on the line. Just sit back and relax." He got to his feet, picked up his pole, attached a worm, cast out, and hit the center of the pond. He grinned when she glared up at him. Then he took a seat on the bank beside her.

****

Piper was having a great time. Although she had to admit when he'd mentioned meeting his daughter, she panicked a little. How would Brooke react to another woman in her father's life? She supposed she'd find out.

Staring out across the pond, she smiled as the sun glistened off it, but the trees surrounding it provided much needed shade. It was a hot day.

As she sat beside Sawyer, she could smell his aftershave, and she wanted to attack the man. He always smelled so good. A tug on her line made her jerk.

"I think I caught a fish," she whispered.

"You don't have to whisper." He laid his pole

140

down and moved closer to her. "Let him run."

"Run where?"

He chuckled. "Just let him take the line for a few seconds. That's right. See the line moving?" He squatted down beside her.

"Yes. How long do I wait?"

"Just wait. Be patient."

"If the line is moving, isn't he hooked?"

"Could be, but if it's not hooked well enough, he'll get off. Fish jump up and get themselves loose."

"Okay." A few seconds went by, and the pole bent as the fish went deeper into the water.

"Now. Jerk the pole hard."

Piper did, then looked at Sawyer.

"Now what?"

"Reel him in. I think you got him," he said.

Piper started reeling in the line, but it was hard since the fish was fighting.

"Oh, my God! He must be huge," she said.

"Keep reeling, Piper. Don't give him any slack. He will do his damnedest to get off that hook."

She laughed. "Look how the pole is bent!"

Sawyer chuckled. "Come on, keep going."

Her arm was getting tired, but she finally got the line closer to the bank. Sawyer stood, picked up the net, and wrapped his hand around the line to pull it in. When he put the net under the fish, he raised it up for her to see, and she deflated like a balloon.

"That's it? That tiny fish? I thought it would be a lot bigger."

"He's about four inches. Small yes, but you caught a fish."

"I'd hate to feel a bigger one on the line."

"I'll take you trout fishing one day. Those fish put

up a hell of a fight."

"Your line is moving," Piper said as she pointed to it.

Sawyer set the net down, moved to his pole, picked it up, jerked it, and reeled in a fish. A much bigger fish than she had caught. He held it up and grinned but cleared his throat when she glared at him.

"I told you the bigger fish were near the center," he muttered.

"What do we do with them?" she asked as she held the pole up with the fish dangling from the line.

"Toss them back. I only catch and release. It keeps the pond stocked. Here, give me your pole."

Piper handed him the pole, watched him remove the fish from the hook, toss it back in, and did the same with his, then he walked to the edge of the pond and squatted down to wash his hands. She laid her pole down, got up, stepped behind him, pushed him into the pond, and laughed as she watched him go under. The laughter died when he came up, shook his head to dispel the water, narrowed his eyes, climbed up the bank, and stalked to her.

"Now, Sawyer, it was just a joke." She turned to run, but he caught her, picked her up, turned back to the pond, and stopped on the bank.

"You really shouldn't have done that, darlin'. Payback is a bitch," he said as he held her over the water.

"No gentleman would throw a woman in there," she said as she wrapped her arms tight around his neck but couldn't stop laughing.

"Well, seeing as I'm no gentleman..." He grinned

and tossed her into the pond.

When she came up from under the water, she heard him laughing, and she swatted her hand on the water, trying to hit him with it. Which really didn't matter since he was already soaked. She frowned up at him.

"Where's your hat?" she asked as she glanced around the pond.

"There," he said as he pointed to the floating hat. "Yours is there." He pointed again to where hers lay on top of the water.

"I'll get them." She swam over to his, then hers, and swam back when something touched her leg, and she screamed. "What's in here? Something touched me."

"Just a fish," he said with a chuckle. "Come on, let me help you out, then we'll saddle up and head back."

"Good thing it's still hot out. This actually feels good," she said and spun around fast in the water when something touched her again. "Get me out of here. I think the little fish I caught has gotten his relatives to gang up on me." She raised her hand to Sawyer. He took it and dragged her up the bank.

****

Sawyer pulled her to him, wrapped his arms around her, and pressed his lips to hers. Piper's arms hugged his waist, and he deepened the kiss. He slowly raised his eyes and stared into hers. He knew he was falling way too fast for this woman.

"Let's get back, take a shower, and head to the diner for dinner after while, if that's all right with you."

It didn't matter that her hair was plastered to her head. She was still the most beautiful woman he'd ever seen.

"Sounds good. I love those burgers."

"Me too. As much as I'd love to take you to Hartland, I don't want you freaking out if Grant shows up." He laughed when she punched his arm.

"He's a celebrity. I've never met one before."

"He's a damn good man."

"It shocked me when I read the article about him and Kay O'Malley. All the rumors about them were finally laid to rest."

"Hell, none of us who know him knew that. They kept it a big secret, but he's happy now with Jessa. In fact, she's the only one Kay would give the interview to."

"You didn't know Kay?"

"No. She was from Kalispell."

"Had you met Kay before the party?"

"Yes. Kay was in their wedding. Grant introduced her. Grant and Jessa are very happy, and Grant's friends are happy for him."

"You went to Grant's wedding?"

"Yes. I told you, I've known him a long time. They had it on his ranch." Sawyer turned to walk to his horse but stopped and tugged at his wet jeans. "I'm not sure how comfortable we're going to be riding back soaking wet."

Piper laughed. "I know, and our shirts are sticking to us too."

He turned to look back at her, and he could see her nipples poking through the material of her T-shirt. Then he raised his eyes to hers. A slow smile lifted her lips, and he was sure his jeans were being tested when she lifted the hem of her shirt, pulled it over her head, then off, and she wasn't wearing a bra. *Holy hell!* She sat down on the blanket, tugged off her wet boots, and got to her feet again. She reached for the snap of her jeans, unzipped them, and pushed them down along with her panties.

When she sat on the blanket again, completely naked, and crooked her finger at him, he practically ran to her. He dropped to his knees, cupped her face in his hands, and pressed his lips to hers as he pushed her to her back.

"God, you are so beautiful, Piper. I want you so much," he murmured against her lips.

"Get those clothes off, Sawyer. I want you too," she said as her fingers combed through his wet hair.

He quickly sat up, pulled his T-shirt off, and stood to remove his jeans. As he shoved them down, he swore when he realized he still had his boots on.

"Shit. You make me lose my head," he said as he sat back down, pulled off his boots, stood, and shucked his jeans while she laughed. He stopped and stared at her. "I don't have my wallet with me. I left it at the house. I'm always afraid I'll lose it when I go riding." He shook his head.

"I'm on birth control, Sawyer, but if you don't feel safe..."

"Oh, baby, I do." He dropped back down to the blanket and moved over her. He spread her legs with his knees and settled between them. He pressed his lips to hers as he moved his hand between them and ran his finger along her slit. She moaned, and he had to clench his jaw to keep from taking her hard and fast.

"Sawyer, please," she murmured.

"I will, baby. I will," he said as he moved his lips across her cheek to her ear then down her neck. He about jumped off the blanket when her hand wrapped around his hard cock, and she guided him inside of her. She tilted her hips, and he thrust hard, making her gasp. "Are you all right? I didn't hurt you, did I?"

"No. No, you didn't. God, you feel so good."

"Not as good as you." He took her lips in a hard kiss and pumped in and out of her. Her legs wrapped around his waist, and he moved harder into her. He knew he wouldn't last. It felt amazing skin on skin with her.

Her breathing increased, and he felt her clench around his cock as she tore her lips from his and cried out his name. He put his face into the crook of her neck as he slammed into her and groaned when he came. He lifted his head and looked into her eyes and grinned when she smiled up at him.

"That was wonderful," she said, sounding breathless.

Sawyer kissed her lips. "Yes, it was."

He rolled onto his back and tried to catch his breath. He knew he was so close to falling for her, but he didn't panic, and that surprised him. She rolled to him, and he wrapped his arms around her. He kissed her forehead, and they stayed there for a while.

"I think we need to get back," she said in a sleepy voice. "I could take a nap."

Sawyer chuckled. "Me too. Let's get going. We'll grab a shower, take a nap, and head for the diner.

"Sounds good." Piper got to her feet and dressed. She turned to look at him, and he watched her frown. "Do you plan on riding back naked?"

He laughed. "I don't think that would be at all comfortable for me. I liked watching you." He got to his feet and dressed. The wet material of the jeans made it difficult to pull them on, but he finally did. He picked up the saddle blanket from the ground, tossed it onto Tabasco's back, and then the saddle. He saw Piper out of the corner of his eye, doing the same with Frick. He mentally shook his head. Marcia always expected him to saddle her horse then cool it down because she was too damn lazy to do it herself. Not that she rode a lot. She always made excuses not to go when he'd ask.

After attaching the tack, he vaulted into the saddle, turned to look at Piper, and grinned when he saw her already on her horse.

****

The following week, Piper sat at her desk at work when her cellphone buzzed. She picked it up to see a text from Sawyer.

"Brooke is here. Can you come for dinner at six tonight?"

Piper nibbled on her bottom lip. She wanted to meet Brooke, but she wasn't sure of the welcome she'd get. Was Brooke going to like her or snub her because of her mother?

She took a deep breath and sent him a text telling him she'd be there and smiled when he sent a text back telling her he couldn't wait to see her. Piper placed her phone down and stared at it. She couldn't wait to see him either, but his daughter was a whole other matter.

"She's twenty-two. She can't be expecting her parents to get back together," Piper murmured. She hoped not anyway, or she'd be getting the cold shoulder for sure.

Cold Shoulder? What a damn understatement. Brooke glared at her practically through the entire dinner. She was a beautiful young woman with her dark hair and tall, statuesque frame, but it was apparent she didn't like Piper at all. Piper had tried to be nice, but Brooke would cut her off. Anytime Piper tried to talk with Sawyer, Brooke would interrupt and ask her father a question. If Sawyer noticed, he said nothing and that pissed Piper off even more.

She sat back in the chair and shifted her eyes back and forth between father and daughter. They were having a grand ole conversation, and it was as if she didn't even exist. As if she wasn't sitting right here with them. She could feel her temper rising, and she tried her best to squelch it, but it took hold. She placed her fork on her plate, making it clang, and both of them turned to look at her. Brooke with a smug look on her face and Sawyer with one of surprise.

"I've had a...*lovely* time, but I need to get up early. I have a meeting," Piper said as she pushed the chair back, picked up her plate, carried it to the kitchen, placed it and her fork in the sink.

"Are you all right?"

She turned around to see Sawyer in the doorway.

"Of course. Why wouldn't I be, Sawyer?" She folded her arms and stared at him.

He huffed, strode to her, and cupped her face in his hands.

"I'm sorry she's being—"

"A bitch?"

"I was going to say childish," he snapped as he dropped his hands from her face.

"You go with that, and I'll go with mine. She is a grown woman, and she will not treat me that way. I'm leaving. Call me when she goes back to Oregon."

Piper pushed past him, walked to the door, opened it, and stepped out.

She pulled her keys from her pocket, aimed the fob at her SUV, climbed in, and tore out of the driveway to head home. A tear rolled down her cheek, and she angrily brushed it away. She refused to cry over this.

****

Sawyer entered the dining room, folded his arms, and stared at his daughter. Brooke looked up at him.

"Happy now?" he growled out.

Brooke shrugged. "If you can't take the heat—"

"Just stop right there. How dare you treat Piper in that manner? I raised you a lot better than that."

"I don't like her," she said.

"You don't even know her," Sawyer shouted and watched as Brooke shoved her plate away and got to her feet.

"And I don't want to. I can't accept another woman in your life! I won't. You belong with Mom."

"Well, let me tell you something, Brooke, it's none of your business who is in my life, and it will never be your mother again. I don't give a rat's ass if you don't like Piper, but you will treat her with respect. You understand me?"

"I won't come around if she's here."

"Quit acting like a child! You're a grown woman."

"Daddy, how can I see you with another woman? You and Mom were married my entire life practically, and neither of you will tell me why you divorced. If I'm a grown woman, why can't you tell me?"

"It's none of your business why we divorced, but if you have to know, ask her."

"I have. She won't tell me either."

Sawyer blew out a laugh. "I wonder why. This is not getting us anywhere. I'll be lucky if Piper ever speaks to me again. I like her. A lot, and I'm telling you, you had better not have screwed this up for me."

He picked up his plate and carried it to the kitchen but stopped alongside her.

"I love you, Brooke, but I will not have you trying to sabotage any relationship I have." He kissed her temple. "Now clean your plate, and load the dishwasher. I have paperwork to do."

After he put his plate in the sink, he strode down the hall to his office, took a seat behind his desk, and turned on the computer. As he stared at the screen, all he could think of was the hurt in Piper's eyes. With a deep sigh, he took his cellphone from his shirt pocket and called her.

"Sawyer?" she said when she answered.

"I'm sorry, Piper."

"You have no reason to be sorry. You did nothing wrong."

"Apparently, I didn't raise my daughter well enough," he said.

"I don't believe that. She's just upset that you and Marcia aren't together any longer."

"I get that, but like you said, she's a grown woman, and her mother and I have been divorced three years. I told her she was acting like a child. I'm sure she's not happy with me right now."

"Probably not. Sawyer, I like you, and I love spending time with you, but if she's going to come between us—"

"That will not happen. It's my life, Piper. Not hers."

150

stopped and checked each one. She stopped in the middle of the aisle, put her hands on her hips, and called out for the dog again. She spun around when she heard a noise and blew out a relieved breath when she saw Rio entering the barn. He stopped alongside her, and she rubbed his head.

"Where's your girlfriend, Rio?"

The dog looked away from her to the open doors at the other end of the barn, back to her, and trotted to the doors.

Piper didn't have a good feeling about any of this. Why would Lola run from her, and why wasn't she coming back when Piper called for her? Had she smelled another animal? A wolf or coyote? She pulled her cellphone from her pocket again and called Sawyer.

"I'm at the house," he said.

"Could she have smelled another animal? Like a wolf or coyote?"

"She could have and ran off to investigate. A dog's sense of smell is amazing. The part of a dog's brain that analyzes smells is about forty times greater than ours. She definitely could have smelled something. I'm heading your way."

Piper sighed as she stuck the phone back into her pocket, then continued to the other end of the barn. She stepped into the sunshine, blinked her eyes from the glare, and quickly glanced to her left when Lola barked. The blood drained from her face as she stared at the one man she hoped would never find her. Cory. And he was holding Lola's collar in a tight grip. Rio stood stock still, staring at him, growling, and the fur on the back of his neck stood straight up.

"Hey, Pip. Are you looking for your dog?" he said

154

"I'm glad, but I will not be at the ranch while she's there. It just creates too much tension."

"Understood. She's only staying a few days, so once Brooke leaves, we'll get together, okay?"

"Yes, but..."

"But what?"

"Is this going to work if we have to stop seeing each other when your daughter is home?"

"I will not stop seeing you. To be honest, I think you coming here would show her you're not backing down."

"You could be right." She said nothing for a few seconds, and he held his breath, waiting, then she spoke. "All right. I've been through worse. I won't let her intimidate me, so I'll be there the next time she visits, but not this time."

"That's my girl. All right, darlin', I'll see you in a few days. Get some rest so you'll be ready for that meeting."

"What meeting?" she said right before she disconnected.

Sawyer stared at the phone, then chuckled. So the meeting had been a ruse to get out of here. He shook his head. Damn, he liked her.

****

The following Saturday, Piper drove to Sawyer's place with Lola in the back seat. The dog seemed to know where she was going because as soon as Piper slowed down to pull into his driveway, Lola started barking.

"Could you not do that next to my ear? I'll be deaf in no time." She laughed when Lola licked the side of her face.

She drove up to the gate to see it closed, so she called Sawyer.

151

"Hey, darlin'," he said in her ear.

"The gate is locked."

"Damn it. I told Brick to leave it open. I'll be right there. I need to get a key made for you. Give me a few minutes, and I'll be there. I'm at the middle barn."

"All right." She put the gear into Park and waited for him. *Get a key made for her? Is that like exchanging house keys?* She snickered at that.

It wasn't long before she saw Sawyer driving a UTV up to the gate. He stopped it, stepped out, and gave her a wave as he sauntered to the gate.

She was so glad she met him. She wiggled in her seat, just thinking of staying with him tonight. She wanted to go over every inch of that man again.

Once he swung the gate open, he waved for her to drive through. She did but stopped beside him and put her window down. He laid his arms on the door and stared in at her.

"Hey, cowboy," she said.

He touched the brim of his hat. "Ma'am."

She laughed. "I'm here to see the doctor."

"Well, I'm sure he'd love to see you too." He leaned in and kissed her lips.

Lola barked from the back seat, and Sawyer reached in and rubbed her ears.

"Hey, big girl." He looked at Piper. "You can go on up to the house. It's not locked. I'll be there in a few minutes."

"All right. Make sure you are." She put the window back up and drove up to the house.

After arriving, she parked by the steps and got out. She opened the vehicle's back door, and Lola jumped out, looked to the barn, and took off running.

152

"Lola," Piper yelled, but the dog kept runn[ing] "Damn it."

She ran in the direction Lola had but didn't her anywhere, so she called her name again. didn't understand. The dog usually listened to and she'd been here before, so Piper didn't get she ran off. She stopped and pulled her cellph from her pocket and called Sawyer.

"I'm on my way," he said when he answered.

"Lola took off. I can't find her."

"Damn, well, she couldn't have gotten far. Ch inside the barn since the doors are open. She m[ight] have gone in there."

"All right," she said in a low tone of voice.

"Piper, baby, it will be fine. She's j[ust] misbehaving today," Sawyer said, and she co[uld] hear the smile in his voice.

"I hope so. She never runs off, and anytime I c[all] her name, she comes to me."

"I'm just about there. If you don't find her befo[re] I get there, we'll look for her together. Don't pan[ic] sweetheart. Like I said, she couldn't have gotten fa[r] Sometimes dogs just take off. Rayna's dog did on[ce] and she never figured out why, but Trick found t[he] dog, and he was fine. It's just what they do times."

Piper huffed out a breath. "Okay, I'm heading f[or] the barn now."

"All right. I'll meet you there." He disconnected

Piper stuck the phone back into her pocket, the[n] walked down the dirt road to the barn.

"Lola," she yelled out.

When she entered the barn, she stopped to l[et] her eyes adjust, then proceeded down the aisle. Th[e] horses were out, so the stall gates were open. Sh[e]

153

with a sneer.

"Cory, let her go," Piper pleaded. God! She really hated it when he called her *Pip*.

"I know she means a lot to you. I've been watching you."

Piper suppressed a shiver as she stared at him. She despised this man, and he had her dog. Lola kept lunging, but he had a firm grip on the collar. Rio didn't move a muscle.

"How did you find me?"

"I remember how you talked about this town after you came here on vacation. You even said you'd move here if you had the chance. You got that chance when you left me, didn't you, Pip?"

"I vacationed in Spring City, not Clifton," she snapped.

Cory shrugged. "I know, but this was the town that impressed you, and now I can see why. You wanted to fuck a cowboy. You whore," he snapped. "I saw you in the field, spreading your legs for him."

"Please let her go, Cory." Piper ignored his words. The thought of him watching her with Sawyer made her sick to her stomach, but there was no way she'd let him know.

"I don't think so. You and I are going to talk. By the way, where's your cowboy now?"

"I'm right here, jackass," Sawyer said as he stepped out from the barn.

Piper watched as he folded his arms, leaned against the barn, and stared at Cory. She looked at Cory to see him swallow hard.

"This doesn't concern you," Cory sneered.

"Well, you just asked where I was, plus you're on my land, so I think it does concern me." He glanced at Piper. "You all right?"

155

"Yes. He doesn't scare me anymore. I just want Lola back."

"How the hell did you get on my property?" Sawyer asked when he looked at Cory.

"Not that it matters, but going under that wire you have strung up is no big deal. She belongs to me," Cory said as he pointed at Piper.

Sawyer chuckled. "Really? I don't believe she thinks the same way as you." He looked at Piper again. "Do you?"

"No."

"See? Take it like a man and let her go. I've already called the sheriff, and he's on his way—" He stopped when he heard the sirens. "Looks like he's right on time."

Piper watched as Cory glanced back and forth between them. Then he let go of Lola, turned, and took off running. Sawyer ran after him with Rio behind him while Lola ran to her.

"Sawyer, stop, please. He could hurt you or Rio. Please," Piper called out and sighed when Sawyer halted and yelled *no* at Rio. When she saw Sawyer stop and turn around to head back to her, she collapsed onto the ground and wrapped her arms around her dog as tears rolled down her cheeks. That monster had found her.

Chapter Seven

Sawyer watched her fall to the ground and ran to her. When he reached her, he squatted down and pulled her into his arms. She cried against his shoulder.

"It's okay, baby. He's gone."

Rio and Lola tried to get as close to them as they could.

"He'll be back. He said he's been watching me, which means he knows where I live and work. He won't stop, Sawyer. He'll do all he can to get to me."

"I won't let him," he whispered and kissed the top of her head.

"You can't be with me all the time." She grabbed fistfuls of his shirt and cried into it.

He rubbed her back and let her cry. He wasn't sure what he could do to make her feel better. This is what she'd been fearing.

"You should have let me, or Rio go after him. Rio would have caught him," Sawyer whispered.

"No. You don't know what he's capable of. He wouldn't hesitate to hurt either of you, and I'd hate for something to happen to you or Rio because of me," Piper whispered.

"Sawyer?"

He glanced up to see Sam with his weapon drawn and Deputy Brody Morgan behind him.

"He's gone, Sam. He took off that way." Sawyer pointed over his shoulder.

The men lowered their weapons and put them in the holsters.

Sam squatted down and touched Piper's shoulder.

"Did he hurt you, Piper?" he asked her.

"No, but he'll try."

Sawyer and Sam looked at each other.

"Do you want me to look, Sam?" Brody asked.

"Yes, and have Betty Lou call in Paul and Mark. Also, get Rick out here. We'll look around. Maybe we can get an idea of what direction he went."

Piper sat up. "You won't find him. He had this all planned out. He may be an abuser, but he's not stupid."

"I'd rather you didn't go home tonight," Sam said to her.

"She'll stay with me," Sawyer said.

"Good. She needs to be kept safe. I'll call Bonner and let him know to look out for him. I'm sure he'll know if someone has been around. Did you lock your place when you left, Piper?"

"I'm not really sure, Sam. I usually do." She shook her head, and more tears rolled down her cheeks.

Sam straightened up, removed his cellphone from his pocket, and Sawyer listened as he spoke to Bonner, then he ended the call.

"Bonner is going to check out the cabin, but I told him not to enter or touch anything," Sam told them.

"I'll need clothes, Sawyer. I have to go to work."

"Can you take a leave of absence?" Sam asked her.

"No. We're too busy. What am I going to do?"

"I'll take you to work and pick you up. You have security guards there, don't you?" Sawyer asked her.

"Yes."

"I'll get them a photo of him so they can keep an eye out for him, but I doubt he'd go inside the hospital. He'll hang around outside so he can—" Sam quit talking.

"Grab me," she whispered.

"It's a possibility. We'll do all we can to protect you, Piper. I'll call Gray too. That way, he can watch for him." Sam glanced over his shoulder when he heard sirens. "Looks like the rest of my deputies are about here. We'll look around. Maybe find some footprints."

"Thanks, Sam," Piper whispered.

Sawyer helped her up and put his hand out to Sam, who took it.

"We appreciate this, Sam."

"It's our job. We'll spread out and see what we can find, then I'll get in touch with Gray and the hospital. I'm just glad you only work daylight hours." Sam touched the brim of his hat, and strode down through the barn. When his deputies entered, he stopped to talk with them.

Sawyer watched as they all walked out the other end, but a few minutes later, they came striding through the barn carrying rifles with scopes. Sam gave him a nod as he passed between him and Piper. Then the men followed him toward the woods where Cory had disappeared.

Sawyer wished he could have caught him, but he had heard the panic in Piper's voice, and knew he had to stop. He should have let Rio go after him, though. There was no way he could outrun a dog. Sawyer was sure that Piper was right, and Cory wouldn't hesitate to hurt Rio if given a chance.

"Come on, baby, let's get you to the house. He

159

won't get close to you there," Sawyer said as he held onto her. He could feel her shaking.

She wrapped her arms around him. He pulled her tight against him and kissed the top of her head. She looked up at him with tears spiking her lashes.

"I need to get clothes, Sawyer. I'd rather go now since I know he can't be close to the cabin."

He kissed her lips. "All right, baby. Whatever you want. Let's get the dogs in the house, then I'll drive you there, and you can pack."

"I'm so scared." She put her face against his neck.

"I know. As long as I'm with you, he will not get close. I promise you that. Let's go."

****

A few minutes later, they drove onto Caroline's Dream, past the house and up the road to the cabin. Piper sat forward when she saw that Bonner's truck was here, then he came from around the back of the little home.

Sawyer pulled up close to the cabin and stopped. Piper opened the door, stepped out, and walked to Bonner. She could tell by the look on his face that something was wrong.

"Bonner?"

"I'm not sure you should go inside, Piper. I looked in the windows, and he tore the place apart. I called Sam, and he's on his way. He'll have to process the crime scene," Bonner said.

"Son of a bitch," Sawyer muttered and looked at Bonner. "Did you see anything outside?"

"He got in through the bathroom window by cutting the screen. There are footprints all around the property. I didn't step in them, but I think it's

160

best if we just sit here and wait for Sam."

"I agree." Sawyer pulled Piper against him. "Did you check the door, Bonner?"

"No. Sam told me not to touch anything."

"I hate Cory," she whispered.

"I'm not too fond of him right now either," Sawyer said as he kissed the top of her head.

"You can stay with us if you'd like, Piper," Bonner said.

"She's going to stay with me." Sawyer hugged her tighter.

"Thank you, though, Bonner."

"Yes, ma'am." A siren could be heard in the distance. "Sounds like Sam's on his way."

They turned to see a sheriff's vehicle coming up the road, then stopped by the house. It wasn't Sam's SUV, though. Piper didn't know this deputy.

"Rick, how are you?" Sawyer asked him.

"Good. You all right?" the deputy asked her.

"Not really."

"I understand that, ma'am. I'm Deputy Rick Stark." He touched the brim of his hat. "I'll be out as soon as I can. I need to get my kit from the cruiser."

Piper watched him walk back to the vehicle, open the trunk, and then appear with a satchel and a camera.

"Once I'm finished, you can get whatever you need. Go down to Bonner's and get some coffee. This will take me a while."

"Good idea," Bonner said.

"Yeah, let's do that," Sawyer said as he led her to his truck.

Piper nodded. She knew Cory would find her, but she thought she'd have more time before he did. Did this mean she needed to run again? She glanced over to Sawyer. Lord, she hated the thought of leaving this man, but what choice did she have? Cory would never give up until he caught her and killed her.

As she sat at the table in the kitchen of Bonner and Stephanie's home, she stared into her coffee cup. She jerked when Sawyer touched her hand, and she looked at him.

"It shouldn't be much longer," he said, and she could see the concern in his eyes.

"I know."

"You're more than welcome to stay here, Piper," Stephanie said.

"She'll be fine at my place." Sawyer squeezed Piper's hand. "Unless you'd rather stay here. I can still come by and take you to work and pick you up. I don't want to pressure you into staying with me."

"No, I want to stay with you," Piper whispered.

"All right."

A knock at the door startled all of them. Piper watched Bonner blow out a breath, walk to the door, peer out, open it, and Deputy Stark entered.

"You can go in now. I have to warn you it's a mess. He really did all he could to tear it up."

"Any fingerprints, Rick?" Sawyer asked.

"Plenty. It's as if he didn't care if we caught him."

"Because all he cares about is getting to me. I ran out on him. He won't let that go." Piper reached for her coffee cup and tried to pick it up, but her hand was shaking too much, so she set it back down.

Sawyer pushed the chair back and stood. She looked up at him.

"Come on, we'll go get your clothes, then head to

my place. Bonner, Stephanie, thank you for the coffee."

"You're more than welcome," Stephanie said.

Piper scooted the chair back, got to her feet, and looked at Stephanie.

"I'm sorry I wasted a cup," she whispered.

Stephanie stepped closer to her and pulled her into a hug.

"Don't worry about it. Please know that we're here if you need us. For anything."

Piper nodded. "Thank you." She looked at the deputy. "Thank you, Deputy Stark."

"Yes, ma'am. You call us if you need anything. We don't care what time it is. We'll be here for you."

"Thanks, Rick." Sawyer shook his hand then led Piper out to his truck.

She was on automation as she climbed into the truck, put her seatbelt on, and leaned her head back as tears rolled down her temples. She heard Sawyer get in the truck, but she couldn't look at him. How could she leave him? She loved him. She gasped and sat up.

"Are you all right?"

Piper looked over to him, then nodded. "Yes. I'm just nervous."

"They'll catch him. He has to know now that you'll have protection."

"I suppose, but he won't care. He'll die happy if he gets to me first," she murmured but didn't say more.

Sawyer drove the truck up to the cabin, parked the truck, and glanced over to her.

"You ready?"

"No."

"I'd get your clothes, but I don't know what you

need. If it were up to me, you wouldn't get any at all. I like you naked."

She looked over at him and saw him trying not to grin. She shook her head.

"I can't go to work naked, Sawyer."

"Right, so we're getting work clothes only," he said with a wink.

She sputtered out a laugh. "Thank you for that. I needed to laugh."

He put his hand under her hair and wrapped it around her nape.

"I promise you, as long as I'm with you, he won't get close. How about learning how to handle a gun now?"

Piper stared at him. She wasn't sure she could shoot anyone, not even Cory, but it might scare him off if she aimed it at him. She nodded.

"Yes."

Sawyer grinned. "Good. We'll work on that tomorrow. Nothing to it. I have a Glock 17 9mm handgun I'll teach you with. It's not heavy since it's made with polymer."

"I don't know what any of that means," she said.

He chuckled. "Glock is the brand, seventeen is the model number, and it's a nine-millimeter, which is the caliber. None of that matters. What matters is that you learn how to use it. You don't have to shoot him, but if he sees that weapon, it should be enough to scare him away."

"That's what I'm thinking." She took a deep breath, opened the door, and looked at Sawyer. "Let's do this."

"Yes, ma'am."

She met him at the front of the truck and smiled when he took her hand. She was glad for the support. They climbed the steps and stopped at the door. Sawyer reached out and opened it. Piper stepped across the threshold and gasped at the mess.

"Son of a bitch," Sawyer muttered.

The cabinet doors stood open, and nothing was on the shelves. Every dish was on the floor, broken into pieces. Cory had even broken her spice bottles. They were scattered all over the floor.

She blinked her eyes to stop the tears, but one rolled down her cheek, and she angrily wiped it away. She refused to cry over him. She'd done that enough when they were together.

Piper slowly made her way to the living room and stood looking at the furniture in shock. He had cut the sofa cushions and pulled the stuffing out, and scattered it across the floor. Shaking her head, she headed down the hallway to her bedroom but stopped by the bathroom and peered in. Nothing was damaged in there, so she moved on down the hall. She stopped outside the bedroom door.

"I'm not sure I can go in there," she whispered.

"I will. Stay here," Sawyer said as he pushed the door open and entered the room. She heard him swear.

Drawing in a deep breath, she entered the room and came to a stop. Her clothes lay scattered all over the floor. The closet was bare, and all the drawers were open on her dresser. When she looked at the bed, she fell to her knees. Cory had slashed the mattress and her bedclothes, but it was the afghan her aunt had made for her that broke her heart. Sawyer squatted down beside her and wrapped his arms around her while she cried.

"Aunt Evie made this for me right after I moved

here. I had to leave the other one behind," Piper whispered.

"If he was standing in front of me right now, I'd kill him with my bare hands," he growled out.

"He's a monster," she said.

"Yes. Can you get up, baby? I'll help you find what you need, and then we'll get the hell out of here."

"This is my home, Sawyer, and now he has made me afraid to even be here."

"I know, darlin'. Once he's caught, we'll get it cleaned up. I don't think there's any sense in trying to straighten it up with him still out there. Who knows when he could come back?" Sawyer stood, put his hand out to her. She took it, and he helped her up.

Once they packed enough clothes for her, Sawyer picked up the two suitcases, and they walked out. She hoped Sam caught Cory, and soon.

****

The next week, there was no sign of Cory anywhere. Sawyer watched as Trevor and Brick led a horse in a pool against a current. His mind was on Piper, though. She wasn't coping very well with Cory being out there. She woke up screaming last night, and he held her while she cried herself back to sleep. He wished he knew what to do to help her. If he had any idea where to look for Cory, he'd track him down, beat the hell out of him, and drag him to Sam.

Sawyer had taken her to work this morning just like he had the past week, but she seemed a million miles away, and it scared him. She had told him one night that she knew she'd have to run again. He tried to tell her she was safe with him, but it didn't seem to matter.

With a deep sigh, he glanced at his watch then up to Trevor.

"I have to go pick up Piper. Once you two finish with this horse, just take off. The rest can wait until Monday. Have a good weekend," he said to them and turned to walk away.

"Boss?"

Sawyer turned back around. "Yeah?"

"Is she all right?" Trevor asked him.

"I don't know, Trev. I really don't."

Trevor nodded. "We're still watching for him."

"I know, and I appreciate it. Maybe he left for now. We can only hope."

"It's been over a week, and no one has seen him. Maybe he did leave."

"Maybe, but if he did, I have no doubt he'll be back. I'll see you Monday."

Sawyer strode from the barn and out into the sun. It was late in the day but still hot. He climbed into his truck, then tore out of the driveway to head for the hospital. It was hot as hell inside the cab of the truck, so he put the window down to circulate some air until the air conditioning blew cooler.

Since the gate was open, he drove on out to the road then to Clifton Memorial. As he pulled up close to the doors, he parked and waited for Piper to come out.

After a few minutes, he glanced at his watch and wondered where she was. Reaching into the pocket of his T-shirt, he pulled his cellphone out and called her, but she didn't answer, and his heart hit his stomach.

"Damn it," he muttered as he shut the truck off then ran to the doors of the hospital. The double doors whooshed open, and he entered the lobby and glanced around.

"Sawyer."

He spun around to see Piper walking to him, and he gave a relieved sigh.

"Darlin', you scared the hell out of me," he said as he pulled her into his arms.

"Why?"

"Why? Because I've been here a few minutes, and when you didn't come out or answer your phone, I panicked."

She looked at her watch. "It's only a minute after five."

He glanced at his watch. "I have almost ten after."

"Your watch is fast," she said with a smile.

"Hell. Why didn't you answer your phone?"

"I just got out of a meeting. I had it turned off."

When she bit her lip, he narrowed his eyes at her.

"You think that's funny?"

"Yep."

Sawyer chuckled. "I think I need a watch battery. Come on, darlin', let's go home."

They walked outside, and he opened the passenger door for her and held her hand while she climbed in. After she pulled the seatbelt on, he leaned in and kissed her lips.

"How about dinner tonight in Hartland?"

"I'd love it." She took her bottom lip between her teeth. "Do you think there's any chance Grant will be there?" She burst out laughing when Sawyer growled low in his throat, slammed the door closed, and strode around the front of the truck. He opened the driver's door, slid onto the seat, looked over at her, and winked.

****

No one saw Cory at all by the time fall arrived, but Piper knew he'd be back. He wouldn't give up on getting to her. She sat in one of the rocking chairs on the front porch and stared at the beautiful colors of the leaves on the trees, and blew out a breath. There was a BOLO out on him, but it was as if he vanished from the face of the earth. *If only.*

"Hey."

She glanced over to see Sawyer standing at the bottom of the steps.

"Hey," she said with a smile.

"I wanted to let you know Brooke is coming next week."

Well, that certainly wiped the smile off her face. She huffed.

"Okay."

"You're staying, right? We talked about this," Sawyer said as he took a seat on the top step.

"I'm not sure I'll be able to hold my tongue though Sawyer if she gets smart with me."

"I don't want you to. She has to understand that I...care about you."

"And if she doesn't?"

He shrugged. "I told you before, Piper, she has no say in my relationships."

Piper nodded and looked to the driveway to see a vehicle coming closer.

"Are you expecting someone?"

Sawyer looked to the driveway. "No-son of a bitch." He got to his feet.

"Who is it?"

"Marcia," he snapped as he walked toward the

169

car but stopped and waited for it to come to a halt.

"Marcia? Oh, this should be good. First the daughter, now the ex-wife," Piper muttered as she watched the door on the car open and a beautiful redhead stepped out. She was impeccably dressed in a black pencil skirt and a green blouse with matching stilettos. And she had more class in her little finger than Piper did in her entire body.

Should she go into the house? She almost burst out laughing when Lola and Rio ran to Marcia, and she tried to hide behind Sawyer. Piper heard Sawyer tell them to go as he pointed to the porch. That was when Marcia noticed her sitting there and headed for her. *Uh oh.* Piper would be damned before she'd get up while this woman barreled down on her.

"Who are you?" she asked Piper.

"Who are you?" Piper threw back.

"I happen to be Sawyer's wife—"

"*Ex*-wife, Marcia. Ex."

Piper bit her lip to keep from smiling when Sawyer winked at her.

"Is this woman shacking up with you, Sawyer?" Marcia put her hands on her hips.

"Shacking up? Seriously, who says that nowadays?" Piper said, making Sawyer bark out a laugh.

Marcia turned to look at her. "You think you're funny, don't you?"

"I am pretty funny."

"Who is she, Sawyer? Besides a smartass?" Marcia turned to look at Sawyer.

"None of your business. Who I...*shack* up with is none of your concern. You need to leave and don't come back. I don't know why you can't get it

170

through your head that it's over between us."

"I said I was sorry," she snapped.

"Sorry just doesn't cut it sometimes. Just how the hell did you get past the gate, anyway?"

"I still have my key," Marcia said with a smug look at Piper.

"Well, I can see it's time to change that lock. Goodbye, Marcia." He walked back to the steps, climbed them, took a seat beside Piper in a rocking chair, and placed his hand over hers.

Marcia glared at Piper, turned around, and opened her car door.

Sawyer got to his feet, walked to the porch's steps, folded his arms, and looked at Marcia.

"Don't come here again, Marcia. Because, so help me if you do, I will have you arrested for trespassing. Since there are signs up, you can't come on this property unless I allow it, and I don't. You are not welcome here. Now go."

Marcia turned around to look at him. "I'm going. You'll never hear from me again. You're making a mistake with this one," Marcia said as she pointed at Piper. "She is not your type at all. She and I are night and day."

"I know, and it's one reason she's in my life. Go," Sawyer snapped.

Marcia glared at Piper one more time and turned to head for her car.

"It was nice meeting you," Piper called out.

Marcia stopped, took a deep breath, got into the car, and tore off down the driveway.

"Why didn't she go to the barn the day she showed up a while back?" Piper asked out of curiosity.

"She wouldn't be caught dead in the barns,"

171

Sawyer said with a grin.

They looked at each other and burst out laughing. It felt so good to laugh again. For weeks, she had been so scared that Cory would get to her. She knew he wasn't around right now, but she also knew he'd be back. He would not give up on getting to her, but it would be a while. Of that, she had no doubt. Not only was he hiding because he was a wanted man, but with colder weather moving in, he wouldn't be out in it. She looked up at Sawyer as he touched her hand, and she smiled.

"One down, one to go," she said with a grin.

Sawyer chuckled. "If you can handle Marcia, you can handle Brooke."

"Marcia is beautiful," she murmured.

"She has nothing on you, baby. You're not only beautiful on the outside but also on the inside. I'm so glad you're in my life."

"She's right, though. We are night and day."

Sawyer took a seat in the chair beside her, took her hand in his, and interlinked their fingers.

"And just like I said, that's one reason you're in my life." He lifted her hand to his lips and kissed her knuckles.

"Maybe I should go back to my cabin now. Cory won't be back for a while."

"What makes you say that?"

"He won't chance coming back with no place to stay, and with colder weather coming, he'll hole up somewhere warm. Probably with a friend or relative in Wyoming. Oh, I know he'll be back, but it won't be for a while. I know him. Trust me on this."

"We'll be ready when he comes back. I believe you're right. He'll be back, but he'll have to go through me." He sighed. "If you want to go back to your cabin, I won't stop you."

"I think I should. Especially with Brooke coming."

"But you'll come here, right?"

"Oh yeah, she will not ruin this for me." She leaned over to kiss his lips.

"Let's go inside. I want you," he said against her lips.

"I want you too."

Sawyer stood, pulled her to her feet, then she laughed when he picked her up, carried her into the house, up the stairs, into his bedroom, and kicked the door closed. He placed her on the bed, took a seat on the side, and toed off his boots.

Piper tugged hers off, threw them to the floor, along with her socks, and removed her T-shirt. She unsnapped her jeans, lowered the zipper but stopped when she saw Sawyer stand, push his jeans down, and turn to look at her in just his boxer briefs. She could see his hard cock straining the material.

She quickly got to her knees, moved close to the edge of the bed, and hooked her fingers into the elastic of his boxer briefs, and tugged him closer. She gazed up into his eyes, pushed them down to his knees, and leaned forward and put her mouth down over his dick. He groaned and gently pulled the band from around her ponytail and combed his fingers through her hair. His hands fisted in it as she sucked on him. His hips moved in rhythm with her mouth sliding down over him and back up.

She wrapped her fingers around him and stroked him as she moved her mouth up and down his length.

"Piper," he said in a gruff voice.

173

Nothing turned her on more than turning on this man. She cupped his balls in her hand and gently kneaded them.

"You have to stop." He tried to pull back from her.

"No, you have taken me over the edge so many times. I want to return the favor."

Sawyer stepped back, took deep breaths, and looked at her.

"Next time. I need to be inside you. I want to fuck you."

She watched him clench his jaw as she wrapped her hand around him again. Their eyes met, and she winked at him, making him grin. He pushed her back onto the bed, grabbed her legs, and pulled her to the edge. He lifted her legs to his waist, moved his finger along her slit, making her wet, then inched into her. She wrapped her legs tight around him as he pounded into her.

"Sawyer, kiss me," she whispered. He leaned over her and took her lips in a hard kiss. She was so close. She needed that orgasm so badly, and she'd beg to get it. "Please," she whimpered.

"Anything for you," he said as he rubbed his thumb over her clitoris, and she tumbled over, screaming his name.

He buried his face in the crook of her neck and groaned as he came. He raised his head and kissed her lips. He fell beside her on the bed then rolled onto his back.

"God, that was good," she said when she could catch her breath.

"When isn't it?"

Piper laughed. "True."

She sat up, ran her eyes over his hard chest to

his six-pack stomach, and back to his face to see him looking at her. She smiled.

"How about a shower? Then we can go into Hartland and have dinner," he said.

"Sounds good to me, cowboy." She slid off the bed, put her hand out to him. He took it, sat up, and got to his feet. He leaned down, kissed her lips, and stared into her eyes.

"You mean so much to me, Piper," he said in a low tone of voice.

"I feel the same, Sawyer." She wanted to tell him she loved him, but she was afraid it was too soon, and he'd panic. "Let's get that shower. I'm anxious to go to dinner."

A week later, she moved back into the cabin. It shocked her that Stephanie and Bonner had cleaned it up for her. They even replaced the furniture and dishware. Piper had cried when she entered the cabin and drove down to their house and hugged them both.

She was happy to be back, but she really wished she could have stayed with Sawyer. She loved him so much, but with Brooke arriving, it was better to be here because Piper knew there would be a lot of tension. She shook her head. How was this ever going to work?

Chapter Eight

Sawyer ran his hand down over his face then around the nape of his neck in frustration, as he watched Piper and Brooke glare at each other. No matter how much he loved these two, it was getting damn ridiculous.

"It doesn't matter if you don't want to go to dinner with us, Brooke. Stay the hell at home. I couldn't care less," Piper growled out.

Brooke looked at him. "Do you see how she talks to me? Are you going to let her do that?"

"*Let her?* He's *your* father, not mine," Piper snapped.

"Just stop you two. Please. You're giving me a damn headache," Sawyer grumbled as he rubbed his temples. When they both started talking at once, he shook his head, turned around, and walked out of the barn.

He stopped, put his hands on his hips, and hung his head. If he didn't get out of there, he'd say something he'd regret. How in the hell was he supposed to have a relationship with Piper if his daughter didn't like her? Brooke had to know that he would not cut Piper from his life just because she was being a child about it. He knew she wanted him and her mother to get back together, but that would never happen.

Raising his head, he glanced over his shoulder at the barn, took a deep breath, turned around, and walked back inside. He didn't see either of them.

He strode down through the barn, looking in

each stall. He found Piper in one of them with Frick. They had kept the horse at his place since Piper would stay with him on weekends even before Cory had found her. She looked over at him, and he could see the hurt on her face.

"Piper..."

She rubbed Frick's neck, walked out of the stall, and closed the gate. She looked up at Sawyer and shook her head.

"She doesn't like me at all, Sawyer," Piper said.

"I don't think it's that she doesn't like you, Piper. She's just not used to seeing me with another woman." He removed his hat, raked his fingers through his hair then resettled the hat on his head.

"You don't *want* to think it's true, but it is. How are we supposed to have a relationship when your daughter hates me?"

"My daughter has no say in my relationships," Sawyer said.

Piper shook her head. "It will eventually kill this."

Sawyer walked away from her, then spun around to look at her, and he watched as she leaned against the wall, slid to the floor, and covered her head with her arms. He was in shock to see her trembling.

Slowly making his way to her, he squatted down and reached his hand out to her.

"Piper. Baby, it's me." She pulled away from him. "I won't hurt you," he whispered.

She raised her head, and tears rolled down her face. He pulled her into his arms and kissed the top of her head.

"I would never hit you."

"I'm sorry—"

177

"You have no reason to be sorry. I guess I scared you when I turned around so fast, but you have to know I would never physically hurt you, and I'll do my damnedest to not hurt you in any way."

"I know. I know. He-he would turn around like that and backhand me. I just had a flashback."

"I'm not him, Piper. Please remember that. We'll have arguments. That's natural. Hitting you isn't."

"Dad? What's going on?"

He looked over his shoulder to see Brooke standing in the doorway. Blowing out a breath, he helped Piper to her feet and wrapped his arms around her.

"Nothing, kiddo."

"Doesn't look like nothing." Brooke stepped forward and peered around him to look at Piper, and then she looked at him. "Dad?"

"It's all right, Brooke. I'm fine," Piper said.

"I'm not stupid. Something happened."

Sawyer blew out a breath. His daughter was nothing if not hardheaded. *Gee, where does she get that?*

"Piper?" he asked.

"My ex-boyfriend abused me," she whispered.

"So why were you on the ground? Did you think my dad was going to hit you? You should know he would never do that," Brooke growled out.

Piper stepped away from him, and her eyes narrowed as she looked at Brooke.

"I do know it, but I had a flashback."

"Brooke, you need to leave right now if you're going to cause problems," Sawyer snapped.

"*I* need to leave? Obviously, *she* thinks you'd hit her," Brooke shouted.

"I'm done. I can't make her like me, and I will not

compete with her." Piper looked at Brooke. "I hope you're happy." Then she turned and stalked out of the barn.

Sawyer spun around to look at Brooke.

"Damn it, Brooke. The one woman I've been interested in since your mother, and you run her off."

"I want you and Mom back together, just like Mom does," Brooke said and folded her arms with a shrug.

"I don't know how many times I have to tell you that will never happen, but you can't seem to get it out of your head," Sawyer said through clenched teeth.

"But why not? You loved her before, Dad, you can again—"

"You need to ask her what happened. Ask her what *she* did, then you come and tell me you want us back together. *It will never happen.*" He frowned. "And instead of jumping all over Piper about her reaction, a little sympathy would have helped. She was in an abusive relationship, and all you could do was make her feel worse about the way she reacted."

"You would never hit her," Brooke shouted.

"She had a fucking flashback, Brooke. Holy shit, show some damn compassion."

Sawyer took a deep breath and strode out of the barn. He was sure Brooke was in shock at the word he'd used, but he was so damn pissed about her acting in that manner, he couldn't help himself.

He had to get to Piper and talk to her. This was not over. No way was he letting her go. He was in love with her. And if Brooke couldn't accept that, it was too damn bad. He deserved to be happy, and

179

he was with Piper. He strode to his truck and drove out of the yard to head for Piper's home. He just hoped she'd talk to him.

****

Piper pulled up to the little cabin, parked then entered the house. Lola sat on the floor, staring up at her.

"Hi, big girl. Do you need to go out?"

Lola ran to the door and waited for Piper to open it. Once she did, Lola ran off the porch, and Piper closed the door. She pulled a chair out from the table, sat down, placed her arms on the table, put her head on them, and cried.

How was this going to work when Brooke hated her? Well, maybe not hate, but she sure didn't like her. Piper knew why Brooke didn't like her. Most children want their parents together, no matter what their age. Brooke didn't know what had happened, and Piper believed she needed to know the truth. Either Marcia or Sawyer needed to tell her. She was twenty-two years old, not a child who couldn't understand.

Lola barked, and Piper got to her feet, looked out the window, and opened the door to let her in when Sawyer pulled up to the house. She stepped onto the porch, folded her arms, and watched him get out of his truck. He sauntered to the steps of the porch, and Lola ran down them to him. He reached down to pet her.

"Piper, I'm sorry."

"You're not the one who should apologize, Sawyer."

"Maybe not, but I'm sorry that Brooke spoke to you in that manner." He stood at the bottom of the steps and looked up at her.

180

"It's all right."

"No, it's not, and she's old enough to know better. Can I come in?"

"Yes, of course." She turned and entered the house, with Lola following.

Sawyer came in behind her, removed his hat, tossed it on the bench, and walked to her. She stared up at him, and a tear slipped down her cheek. He pulled her into his arms.

"Oh, baby. I'm so sorry I scared you." He cupped her face in his hands. "You have to know I'd never hurt you."

"I do know. It was just a reaction."

"I...Piper, I love you," he whispered.

"Oh, Sawyer, I love you too, but—"

"No buts."

"Brooke—"

"She does not have a say in my relationships."

"Maybe not, but she will cause so much tension between us. It's there now. I want to get along with her, and I try, but she acts like she has no desire to even want to get to know me."

"I know, and I'm sorry she's treating you that way. I could have sworn I raised her better than that." He kissed her forehead.

"You should tell her about Marcia."

"I told her to ask her mother why we're divorced. If Marcia doesn't tell her, I will."

"You have to. She's never going to stop wanting you two together until she knows the truth."

"I know. I'll do it tonight. I promise." He kissed her lips.

"Good. Let me know how that goes."

Sawyer blew out a laugh. "Yeah, I will. I have to go. I have a client coming, but I wanted to make sure you were all right. I'll call you later. I do love you so much."

"I'm happy to hear that. I love you too. We'll figure this out."

"Yes, ma'am, we will." He kissed her forehead, picked his hat up from the bench then turned to look at her. "We'll do dinner another night."

"Sounds good."

"I'm sorry she ruined our Saturday night date."

Piper smiled. "There will be others."

"Yes, ma'am." He walked out, closing the door behind him.

****

Sawyer drove home, met with the client, and made plans to get the man's horse to the hospital for therapy. He then drove his truck to his house. Brooke's vehicle was sitting in its usual spot. He parked beside it, took a deep breath, and stepped out. He climbed the steps to the porch, opened the door, and entered the kitchen. Rio came running to greet him. Sawyer took his hat off, hung it on the peg, and rubbed the dog's ears.

"Brooke?" he called out as he walked into the living room.

"Yes?" she asked from where she sat in the recliner.

"I think we need to talk." He took a seat on the sofa and looked at her.

"About what?"

"Come on, Brooke. Stop being childish about this. Piper means a lot to me."

"I don't like her," she said with a shrug.

"You want to tell me why, other than you wanting your mother and I back together."

"I just don't." She shrugged again.

182

"Well, I don't know what to say to change your mind about her. You like her, or you don't. That doesn't concern me. You're old enough to make your own decisions about people, but not liking her because you think your mother and I belong together is just wrong. You're not being fair because you won't even give Piper a chance. You're acting like a spoiled brat instead of a grown woman. Your mother and I will not get back together. I want you to stop even thinking about that."

Brooke sat forward in the recliner and looked at him.

"Mom told me she wants to work it out with you, and I don't understand why you can't, at least, try."

"One reason is that I'm in love with Piper, and the other is one I don't think you want to hear."

"I do, Dad. Maybe if one of you would tell me why you divorced, I'd get it."

Sawyer sat back, glanced around the room, and back at her.

"Your mother had an affair."

Brooke jumped up from the recliner. "I don't believe that."

"Of course, you don't. That's why you were never told. I wouldn't lie about something like that. Now, never suggest we get back together again. It won't happen. It's like beating a dead horse with you over this. When people take those vows, they're supposed to believe in them. I did. Your mother didn't. I love Piper, and I'm hoping she'll marry me, and you might not like her, but you will never speak to her like that again. Are we clear? Because if we aren't, *you* will not be welcome here."

Brooke stared at him, then ran out of the room and up the stairs. He winced when the door slammed. Shaking his head, he pushed to his feet so he could start dinner. He hoped Piper was all right.

As he entered the kitchen, he pulled his cellphone from his pocket and called her. He put the phone on speaker, placed it on the counter, and opened the fridge to look for something to prepare.

"Hey," she said when she answered.

"Are you all right, darlin'?"

"I'm fine. I overreacted today, and I'm sorry. I know you'd never hurt me like he did."

"I'm glad you realize that. He was an ass, Piper. No real man hits a woman. No matter what the reason. If I was that kind of man, I would have hit Marcia when she told me about the affair."

"True."

"I told Brooke."

"How did she take it?"

"Well, she's in her room after slamming the door," he said with a chuckle.

"Uh, oh. It's never good when a woman slams a door."

"Hell, I know that's right."

"She'll get past it. She loves you, Sawyer, you know that."

"I do. I love her too. She's my little girl, no matter how old she gets. I just wish she'd give you a chance."

"Maybe one day when she realizes we both love you."

"I hope so, baby. How about dinner Friday night?"

"Sounds good. I'll see you then. I hear Lola barking, so I have to check on her."

"All right. Keep the gun with you. I'll see you

Friday at six. I love you, Piper."

"I love you too."

Sawyer hit *End* then stared at the shelves in the fridge to look for something to eat. He pulled the drawers open, but nothing appealed to him right now.

"Dad?"

He straightened up and spun around to see Brooke standing in the doorway with tears on her cheeks.

"Yeah?"

"I'm sorry—" she said with a sob.

Sawyer pushed the door closed, strode to her, pulled her close, and kissed the top of her head.

"It's okay."

"No, it's not. I-I talked to Mom. After a good bit of prodding, she told me she had an affair. I was so angry that I hung up on her. I heard you and Piper talking."

"Oh." He didn't know what else to say.

"I can't believe Mom did that."

"I know, kiddo. I just wanted you to know the truth, so you don't keep thinking we could get back together."

"No, I get it. It's going to be hard for *me* to forget that, so I know you won't."

"I won't, but I *am* over it. Piper made me realize that not all women are like your mother, just as I showed her not all men are like her ex."

"I feel so bad for treating her the way I have."

"All you have to do is tell her you're sorry. She'll forgive you. I know she will." He cupped her face in his hands and lifted her face up. "She really is a wonderful woman."

Brooke smiled. "She must be if you love her."

Sawyer grinned. "I love you too, ya know."

"I know, Daddy. I love you too. I just want you happy, and Piper seems to make that happen."

"Yeah, she does. Give her a chance."

"I will." Brooke's head tilted. "Why did you tell her to keep the gun with her?"

Sawyer hesitated to tell her, but he wanted to be honest about it, so he told his daughter about Cory.

"He sounds like a real bastard," Brooke said.

"He is. We're keeping an eye out for him. We're hoping he won't show up until the weather gets warm again."

"I feel so bad for her, and I jumped all over her for..." Brooke shook her head.

"It's okay. You didn't know."

"But when she told me, I shouldn't have reacted that way. I'm so sorry."

"You need to tell her that."

"I will. I'm going to go take a nice hot bath."

"Don't you want something to eat?"

"I ate earlier. You know, like a normal person."

Sawyer growled and pulled her tight against him.

"I don't know what normal is. Go. I'll see you tomorrow. Sleep well, kiddo."

"You too, Dad." She kissed his cheek, turned, and left the kitchen.

Sawyer huffed. He wanted the two women in his life to get along. They didn't have to be best friends, just be kind to one another.

****

The next day, Piper sat on the sofa watching TV when Lola jumped up, stared toward the kitchen, and growled. Piper got up from the sofa and looked at Lola.

"What is it, girl?" she whispered.

She always worried when the dog barked, but to hear her growling was something new. She slowly made her way to the kitchen with Lola on her heels.

At the door, she peered out the window and saw Brooke's SUV. What was she doing here? Was she coming here to tell her to stay away from her father? Piper wasn't sure how she'd respond to that. Maybe just give her the finger and slam the door, she thought with a chuckle.

She opened the door, stepped onto the porch, and waited for Brooke to get out of her vehicle. The driver's door opened, and she stepped out and stared up at her.

"What are you doing here, Brooke?"

"I owe you an apology. I shouldn't have talked to you the way I did, and for that, I'm so sorry. I know Daddy loves you, and you love him. I'm okay with that."

"Seriously?" Piper asked, with skepticism in her voice.

"I figured you wouldn't believe me, but I'm being honest here, Piper. Dad doesn't even know I'm here. I acted like a spoiled brat instead of a mature woman. I wanted my parents back together just as any child does, but I...talked to my mother and got it out of her why Dad wanted nothing to do with her. I'm so pissed at her for destroying their marriage. I don't blame Dad for divorcing her. She messed up a good thing, and I can see why he can't forgive her."

"And what about *you* forgiving her?"

Brooke blew out a laugh. "I seriously don't know if I can right now. I hate how she hurt him."

Piper sighed. "How about coming in for some

coffee?"

"I'd love some."

"Come on in then. Maybe you can tell me things about your dad he doesn't want me to know," Piper said with a grin.

"Oh, I can definitely do that." Brooke walked up the steps, and they entered the kitchen.

Later, as she stood on the porch and watched Brooke drive off, she smiled as she thought about getting to know Brooke better. She wasn't a spoiled brat, as Piper had first thought. She was a lovely, intelligent woman, and Piper hoped a friendship would develop.

As she turned to go back inside, she froze when Lola stood on the porch, growling. Piper looked at her to see the fur on the back of her neck standing straight up.

"Lola, get in the house," she whispered.

Lola glanced at her, back at the woods across the dirt yard, and Piper shivered, but not because of the cold. She knew he was out there. Watching. Waiting.

"Lola, now," she said through clenched teeth, and the dog turned around and entered the house. Piper ran inside, locked the door, and called Sawyer.

"Hey, darlin'," he said when he answered.

"I think he's here," she whispered in a shaky voice.

"I'm on my way. Call nine-one-one. Now." He disconnected.

Piper took her purse off the hook by the door, found Sam's card and called him instead.

"Sheriff Garrett."

"Sam, it's Piper—"

"What is it?" he asked sharply. He could probably hear the fear in her voice.

"I think Cory's here. Please get here. Sawyer's on his way. I'm so scared."

"I know you are. Make sure you lock the doors and windows. I'm heading to my SUV now. I'll be at your place in just a few minutes." He ended the call.

"Oh, God, please hurry, both of you," she pleaded and screamed when she heard a window break.

She rushed to her bedroom, and as she passed the living room, she saw him climbing through the window.

"You can run, Pip, but I will always find you," Cory said as he ran after her.

Lola barked, then Piper heard her yelp. He better not have hurt her dog. She made it to the bedroom, shoved the door closed, and locked it. She backed away from it as Cory kicked at it. It was a thick door, so he wouldn't get in easily, but she also knew he wouldn't stop until he did.

Turning, she ran to the nightstand and got the gun from the drawer. She held it out in front of her with both hands...and waited.

****

Sawyer drove like a mad man to get to her. That son of a bitch better not touch a hair on her head, or he'd kill him. He lowered his window a little when he thought he heard sirens and sighed when he did. And they were getting closer.

"Dear God, please don't let anything happen to her," he prayed.

He pulled his cellphone from his pocket and called Bonner.

"Hey, Sawyer," Bonner said when he answered.

"Piper thinks Cory is at the cabin," Sawyer told him.

"On my way," Bonner told him and disconnected.

"Keep calm, Piper. I'm on my way, baby," Sawyer muttered.

What the hell was all the traffic about? There were never this many vehicles on this road. *Son of a bitch.* He needed to get to her. He knew she had to be scared. That bastard didn't care what he did to her. Sawyer wrapped his hands tight around the steering wheel and clenched his jaw until it ached.

"You hurt her, and you're a dead man."

As he came over a rise in the road, he slammed on the brakes because traffic was at a standstill, and he could see a long line of vehicles in front of him.

"Motherfucker," he yelled and hit his fist against the steering wheel.

He leaned his head back and blinked back tears. He had to get to her. He *had* to. He threw the gear into Park, got out and walked to the vehicle in front of him, and tapped his knuckles on the window. The man lowered the window a little and glared up at him.

"What's going on?" Sawyer asked as he jerked his chin to the line of vehicles in front of him.

"Construction. They're working on the bridge."

"On a Sunday?"

"Yeah, seems they're running behind on getting it done."

"Son of a bitch. I need to get through."

"Good luck with that. If you want to get to the other side of the bridge, you'll have to turn around and take the first dirt road on the right. It's rough, but since you have a truck, you should be fine. If I was in mine, that's what I'd do—"

Sawyer didn't listen to what else the man had to say. He turned around, ran to his truck, got in, did a U-turn, and drove back to the dirt road. He didn't know why he hadn't thought of it. He knew which road it was. *Idiot!*

He floored the truck back to the road, turned right onto it. Rough was a damn understatement, but he put the truck in four-wheel drive and tore down the road. It was a long way around, but he couldn't just sit in traffic. He hoped Sam and Bonner were there already.

****

Piper jerked when the door burst open, and Cory stood in the doorway with a knife in his hand. Blood dripped from it. He laughed when he saw her holding the gun.

"You don't have the balls, Pip," he said as he stood there staring at her.

"Try me," she said. "What did you do to my dog?"

"You don't want to know. I hate dogs," he sneered.

"You better not have hurt her." Piper's hands shook as she held the gun out.

"I don't think you'll save her. She was bleeding all over the fucking place."

Piper blinked back tears. "You bastard."

Cory folded his arms, leaned against the doorjamb, and smirked.

"I've been called worse."

"I called the Sheriff. He's on his way."

"You'll be dead before he gets here, Pip. I can promise you that."

She shivered but refused to let him scare her

anymore.

"You come toward me, and you'll be the one who's dead. I will take great pleasure in shooting you. In fact..." She lowered her aim. "I think shooting you in the balls would be very satisfying." She clenched her jaw when he laughed.

"Since you supposedly called the cops on me, I won't be able to have a little fun with you first. I suppose you called that cowboy you've been fucking too."

"I called him first."

Cory shook his head. "Whore."

"He makes me feel more like a woman than you ever did. He's a good man, something you're not. You fucking coward. You think hitting a woman makes you a man. All it does is make you a coward. Stand up to a man, see where that gets you," she spat the words at him.

She watched as he clenched his jaw. She was so sick of being afraid of this piece of trash. She took a deep breath and raised the gun to his chest, held it steady, and looked him in the eye.

He took a step forward but stopped. He flipped the knife closed, put it in his pocket, and fisted his hands. She knew he was livid that she would talk to him like this. For once in her life, since knowing him, she stood up to him.

"Yeah, just what I thought. You spineless worm."

"I got thinking that you probably didn't expect me back until spring, but this just can't wait any longer. I'm going to kill you and take great pleasure in it."

"You're a sick man-no, not a man. No real man hits a woman. You're a spineless pig, and I am so ready to be rid of you."

192

A smirk lifted his lips as he pulled a gun from the back of his jeans. "You know, you should have taken the safety off if you really planned on using that gun. I know the safety is off this one." He raised the gun.

Piper glanced down to the gun in her hand, and in that split second, he was on her. He shoved her back against the wall, backhanded her with the gun, sending her to the floor, and her gun flew from her hand. He stood over her, and she was way past terrified as she watched him grip the gun in his hand, aimed it at her, and clenched his jaw. She was so stupid for believing him. She *knew* the safety was off.

Glancing around, she saw the gun handle under the bed and reached out for it, but Cory kicked her in her shoulder, making her gasp out in pain. She scooted back to the corner of the wall beside the nightstand on her butt and covered her head.

"You fucking bitch, I *will* kill you this time." He pulled her up by her hair, making her grab his arms.

"Sheriff's department. Let her go. Now," Sam said as he appeared in the doorway.

Piper sighed with relief, but it was short-lived when Cory pulled her in front of him and shot at Sam twice, striking him, and he fell to the floor.

When Sam groaned and moved, Cory dragged her by her hair to where Sam lay. Piper wasn't sure what came over her, but she slammed her foot down on top of his, and when he turned to face her, she used her fist and hit him in the balls. He dropped his gun, grabbed his crotch, staggered back, and fell to the floor. She squatted down, grabbed the gun, got to her feet, backed into the corner, and aimed it at him.

"You're right. The safety is off, Cory. Now get up and try that again, you pussy!" she shouted.

He slowly got to his feet and stared at her.

"You still don't have the balls, Pip. I will kill you where you stand." He reached into his pocket and pulled out a knife, all the while not taking his eyes off her. With a flick of his wrist, the knife snapped open.

"Come and get me," she whispered.

A low growl came from him as he ran at her, and she pulled the trigger. His eyes widened as he looked at her, then down to his chest at see blood oozing out. She blew out a ragged breath when he fell to the floor, but she still didn't move as she stared at him. Her hands started shaking as she lowered the gun.

"Sam? Piper?"

"In here, Bonner," she called out.

"Sam," Bonner said in a shocked voice, and she knew he was checking on his friend. Then he entered the room and quickly called nine-one-one. He stepped over Cory on the floor, kneeled down, and checked for a pulse. He looked up at her.

"He's dead."

She slid to the floor and passed out.

Piper opened her eyes to see Sawyer sitting on the edge of the bed.

"Sawyer?"

He leaned down, put his head on her chest, and she could feel him shaking. She ran her fingers through his hair.

"God, baby, I was so scared he'd get to you before I got here, and he did. I'm so sorry."

She wrapped her arms around his head.

"I'm fine. I'm so glad you taught me how to use that gun." She looked up to see Deputy Morgan beside the bed. "Sam?"

"He's in surgery, but he'll be fine. One hit him in the arm and one in his vest. That vest saved his life, but he'll be sore from that, and knowing Sam, he won't be happy about it." Deputy Morgan grinned.

"I'm so glad he's all right. Cory was dragging me over to where Sam was, and I knew he would shoot him again. I couldn't let that happen. Am I in trouble, Deputy?"

"No, ma'am. It was justified. Sam told me before they put him in the ambulance that he heard it all. We know what he would have done to you if he'd been able to, and going by that bruise on your cheek, he hit you. Also, from where he fell, he was definitely advancing toward you. The knife he had fell next to him." He touched her shoulder. "It's over now. You'll be fine."

"I was outside, but Sam wouldn't let me come in," Bonner said from the doorway with Stephanie beside him. "I had to, though, when I heard the shots."

Stephanie shook her head. "You could have been shot, Bonner Gentry."

Bonner grinned at Piper, then at Stephanie. "I had my gun too, darlin'."

"I'm so glad you're all right, Piper," Stephanie said as she put her arms around Bonner's waist.

Piper nodded as tears ran down her temples. Sawyer raised his head to look at her, and she saw tears on his cheeks.

"I'm sorry I didn't get here in time. I had to backtrack because of road construction." He shook his head.

195

"I'm really all right, Sawyer. He'll never hurt me or anyone else again." She cupped his face in her hands. "I love you."

"I love you too," he said and leaned down to kiss her lips.

"Lola?" she asked when he raised his lips from hers.

"She's fine. Cory stabbed her but missed any vital organs. She lost a lot of blood, but I patched her up. I keep a medical bag in my truck. Rick took her to the hospital in his cruiser with the lights and siren going. The techs will make sure she's comfortable. Tess will check on her when she's able. She's at the hospital with Sam. The techs know they can call me if Lola's condition changes, but she's tough like her mistress."

Piper burst into tears, wrapped her arms around Sawyer, and he pulled her into his arms. She was safe, Lola was fine, Sam would be, Cory was dead, and Sawyer was her life. She'd never have to run. Unless it was to this man.

****

The weather changed in a heartbeat from fall to winter, and snow fell. Sawyer watched as Brooke go down the driveway to head back to school. He waved, then she disappeared. He glanced to Piper to see tears on her cheeks and mentally shook his head.

"Tears? Happy ones because she's gone or sad ones because she's gone?" He chuckled when she swatted at him.

"I'm going to miss her," Piper said.

"Holy hell. For the life of me, I will never understand women."

"We talked things out. She's still hurt by what

196

Marcia did, but she wants you to be happy and says I'm the one who makes you that way."

Sawyer pulled her into his arms and kissed the top of her head.

"You do, darlin'." He leaned back, cupped her face in his hands, and stared into her eyes. "I love you, Piper, and I want to marry you. I want to spend the rest of my life with you. I know you'd never cheat on me, and you know I will never raise a hand to you."

"Oh, Sawyer, I want to marry you too."

"I want you to move in here with me. I don't like it when you're so far away."

"I want that too." She smiled up at him. "It's not like we have to rush into marriage, right? We know we love each other."

"Yes. We definitely know that." He frowned. "Are you all right? I mean, about shooting Cory?"

"Yes. You know I had trouble sleeping the first couple of weeks, but I've gotten better, and I'm glad you taught me how to shoot that gun. I even told him to come and get me."

Sawyer chuckled. "That's my girl. Let's head in and enjoy a snowy day by the fireplace."

"The one in the bedroom?"

"Are there any others?" He raised his eyebrow at her, making her laugh.

Sawyer knew this woman would always be by his side as they walked up the steps to the porch, and into the house. No matter what. He was glad she had stood up to that bully.

Sawyer knew he'd lay down his life for her if it came to it, but he also knew she could take care of herself. He grinned as he led her to the bedroom.

Epilogue

"Are you awake?" Piper whispered next to Sawyer's ear.

"No."

She laughed. "Okay, well, I'm getting up. I need to get the turkey ready to put in the oven."

"Hell, Piper, it's still dark out," he said around a yawn.

"I like to cook it slow."

Sawyer snorted out a laugh. "I like to cook it slow too."

"Stop. You are so bad," she said and snickered.

"Okay, baby, you go do your thing. I'll be down later. I'm tired."

"You know, you keep telling me how old you are, and now I'm beginning to believe it if you can't take a night of lovemaking and get up in the morning."

"Oh, I can get up in the morning. Want to see?"

Piper fell back onto the bed and burst out laughing.

"I have to stuff the bird," she said.

Sawyer laughed. "I could get really crude here, but I won't."

Piper giggled, rolled away from him, moved to the edge of the bed, and got to her feet. She picked up her robe from the rocking chair beside the bed, pulled it on, and tied the belt.

"Go back to sleep. I'll see you later." She leaned down and kissed his lips, then headed out of the bedroom for the kitchen.

She flipped on the lights as she made her way through the house, then entered the kitchen.

After taking the turkey out of the fridge, she placed it on the counter and went about making the stuffing.

After getting the stuffing in the bird, she put it in the oven. She leaned back against the counter and smiled when she heard the pet door flap open and close. She looked over to see Rio and Lola running into the room. Both skidded to a halt, sat in front of her, and stared up at her with silly dog grins on their faces. She squatted down and hugged them.

Lola had made a full recovery thanks to Sawyer stitching her up and Rick quickly getting her to the animal hospital. Piper didn't know what she would have done if Lola had died. She loved the dog so much. With a chuckle, she thought she probably would have shot Cory again. He wouldn't have felt it, but it would have made her feel better. She was just glad that Sam hadn't been seriously hurt or killed. She wasn't sure she'd ever be able to forgive herself if that had happened.

She was finally past the nightmares. Thank God for Sawyer being with her every night. Anytime she woke up, either screaming or quickly sitting up, he would put his arms around her and hold her until she fell back asleep. She would always be thankful to Tess for sending her to Sawyer. That man was her life, and she trusted him with hers.

Piper headed upstairs to change clothes and get ready for the day. It was one Thanksgiving where she truly had a reason to be thankful.

****

Later, when Sawyer woke up, he glanced at the clock to see it was almost nine. He never slept this late. He threw the blanket off, got to his feet, picked up his jeans and T-shirt, and headed for the bathroom to grab a quick shower.

A few minutes later, he entered the kitchen, but it was empty. Damn, the turkey smelled so good. He was hungry. He made himself a cup of coffee and leaned against the counter as it brewed.

"Hey."

He looked to the doorway to see Piper standing there, and he frowned.

"When did you change into your clothes?"

"Not long after I got the turkey in the oven. You didn't even stir while I did."

"You should have gotten back in bed with me," he said and grinned when she blushed.

"Don't think I didn't want to. Everyone should be here in about an hour," Piper said as she moved closer to him. Brooke, Sawyer's father, her parents, and her Aunt Evie and Uncle Drew were all coming to the house.

Sawyer pulled her into his arms, kissed her lips, and then her forehead.

"I know. Want to grab a quickie before they get here?"

Piper laughed against his chest. "You, Dr. Sawyer Griffin, are one horny man."

"Only with you, baby."

"Damn good thing. I know how to shoot a gun, remember?"

"Shit."

She gazed up at him. "Happy Thanksgiving."

"Happy Thanksgiving to you, darlin'."

"I'm so happy everyone can be here. It will be a full house for sure," Piper said with a smile.

He took her hand in his. "Come into the living room with me."

"I'd go anywhere with you."

Sawyer looked at her and winked. "I'm happy to hear that."

They entered the living room, and the enormous Christmas tree in the front window made him smile. Piper had insisted on having it up by Thanksgiving, and he was glad he'd let her talk him into it. It really was beautiful, and the snow falling outside the window behind it made it even more so. He led her to the sofa and had her sit.

"Aren't you going to sit down with me?" she asked him with a frown on her beautiful face.

"In a minute." He walked to the tree, kneeled down, and reached under it to around the back. He pulled the little package out, stood, then walked back to her.

Piper stared up at him, looked at the package in his hand, and back up at him.

"Sawyer?"

He dropped to one knee in front of her. "Piper, I told you I wanted to marry you, and I was going to wait until Christmas, but I can't. I want this on your finger now." He handed her the gift. "Open it."

She stared at the box, then looked at him. He could see the tears in her eyes, and he panicked. What if she wasn't ready for this? He huffed out a sigh when she tore the paper off then looked at the black velvet box. He removed it from her hand, opened the lid, and heard her gasp when she saw the three-carat princess-cut diamond ring with a platinum band. He took the ring out of the box, lifted her left hand then looked into her eyes.

"Piper Howard, I have never loved anyone as much as I love you. Will you marry me?"

She put her hand over her mouth as tears rolled

down her cheeks, and she nodded her head. He grinned, slid the ring on her finger then kissed her knucklcs. He leaned forward to kiss her, but she threw herself at him, and they tumbled to the floor. Rio and Lola jumped around them, barking.

"Aren't you going to say anything?" he asked against her lips.

"I'm speechless," she whispered.

"Hell, I know that's a lie," he said and laughed when she punched his arm.

"I love you, Sawyer." She rolled off him, onto her back, lay on the floor, and held her hand up to look at the ring. "It's so beautiful."

"I did good, huh?"

"Yes, you did. I hope Brooke is okay with this," she said and nibbled on her bottom lip.

"I already told her I was asking you. She's thrilled."

Piper stared up at her hand. "It's just so gorgeous."

"Just like you."

Sawyer got to his feet, pulled her up, and kissed her lips.

"Let's go celebrate. Everyone won't be here for a while yet," Piper said against his lips.

"Darlin', you read my mind." He picked her up, tossed her over his shoulder then took the stairs two at a time. He entered their bedroom and kicked the door closed. They both laughed when the dogs barked. They needed to get used to it, he thought as he headed for the bed. He hoped they did because he planned on getting this woman, the love of his life, in bed as much as possible. He wanted to show her he would always cherish her and treat her as a man should treat the woman he loved.

He tossed her onto the bed, lay down beside her, and took her lips in a deep kiss. His heart was so full of love for her he wondered how he'd been before she came into his life. But he knew that he'd never have to wonder about that. He knew she'd stay by his side, and he'd be right alongside her. Through thick and thin, and anything *anyone* tried to throw their way. They'd be ready, and Sawyer knew he'd protect her with his life if it came down to it. No one would take her from him. He raised his head and stared into her eyes to see tears in them, and he had to blink back tears of his own.

"I love you. We'll have a great life together," she whispered as she cupped his cheek in her hand.

"Damn right we will," he said.

"I'll be happy as long as you're beside me."

"It's where I'll always be. Now, we have an hour. Let's put it to good use," he said with a grin.

Piper laughed. "Sounds good to me, cowboy."

Sawyer stared into her eyes, then lowered his lips to hers. He was happy to have this woman's love. Life was good and always would be as long as she was beside him.

The End

About the Author

Susan was born and raised in Cumberland, MD. She moved to Tennessee in 1996 with her husband, and they now live in a small town outside of Nashville, along with their three dogs. She is a huge Nashville Predators hockey fan. She also enjoys fishing, taking drives down back roads, and visiting Gatlinburg, TN, her family in Pittsburgh, PA, and her hometown. Although Susan's books are a series, each book can be read as a standalone book. Each book will end with a HEA and a new story beginning in the next one. She would love to hear from her readers and promises to try to respond to all. You can visit her website, Facebook page, Instagram, and email by the links below.

www.susanfisherdavisauthor.weebly.com

Susan Fisher-Davis, Romance

Author | Facebook

Susanfisherdavis_author

Email: susan@susanfisherdavisauthor.com